MW01121923

the truth
be told

a novel

the truth be told

a novel

E. Louise Jaques

Jan-Carol
Publishing, Inc
"every story needs a book"

The Truth Be Told
A Novel
E. Louise Jaques

Published January 2018
Little Creek Books
Imprint of Jan-Carol Publishing, Inc
All rights reserved
Copyright © 2018 by E. Louise Jaques
Front Cover Design: Kristen Chumley Jaques
Book Design: Tara Sizemore

This book may not be reproduced in whole or part,
in any manner whatsoever without written permission,
with the exception of brief quotations within book reviews or articles.

ISBN: 978-1-945619-51-9
Library of Congress Control Number: 2018931947

You may contact the publisher:
Jan-Carol Publishing, Inc
PO Box 701
Johnson City, TN 37605
publisher@jancarolpublishing.com
jancarolpublishing.com

To Mike, my true love and best friend. Your love, support, and encouragement have been the foundation of my life for 45 years. You're an amazing father, and soon will be a wonderful grandfather.

To our incredible children—and my editors—Matt Jaques, Becky Jaques Hasak, and Tom Jaques. I'm so proud of the kind, compassionate, enlightened adults you are today. I'm so excited for the next chapters of your lives, as you marry and have children. You'll be outstanding parents!

A special thank you to Kristen Jaques for the concept and design of the brilliant book cover. Your creativity and talent continue to amaze me.

In memory of our parents, Walter & Madeleine Jones and Dudley & Mary Jaques, and my high school friend, Linda Lees.

CHAPTER 1

The Coming Storm

A melia, look behind you! There's a pod of dolphins."
Amelia Jones teetered on her paddleboard. She turned to see the glorious, silver-grey bottlenose dolphins rise above the surface of the ocean, then slip beneath the tranquil water. She steadied herself and laughed with her friend Lyla, as they guided their boards away from the pod.

"That's amazing! I'm loving island life," Amelia said.

"Are we crazy to try stand-up paddleboarding at our age?" Lyla asked. "This is harder than I thought. But not bad for our first time."

"Fifty-eight isn't so old. You're still in great shape. Me, not so much! I'm glad I'm finally trying new things."

"We could both use a little adventure." Lyla added, "It's too bad that Ruby couldn't join us."

"Maybe next time."

The ladies looked toward the miles of white sand beach dotted with colorful chairs and umbrellas, then paddled further out in the ocean. Massive, billowing clouds filled the azure sky to the south of Amelia Island, Florida, located on the eastern Florida-Georgia border.

The women had become instant friends when they met two years earlier at a newcomer's event. They bonded over the challenge of being empty nesters, and their love of good books and great wine. They were attracted to the island by the beauty of the Lowcountry marshlands, the majestic oaks draped in Spanish moss, and the abundant wildlife. The friendly locals and unpretentious new residents were also a factor.

When the breeze began to pick up, Amelia gazed north and saw threatening dark clouds moving quickly in their direction. She'd been caught in an unexpected downpour the week before, and didn't want to experience the wild, driving rain again.

"The storm's coming in fast. Let's head back," Amelia called out as she turned her board toward the shore. They paddled hard against the rising waves, struggling to stay upright. Suddenly, a roar came out of the sky. Two Navy helicopters swung low over the water and sped north toward the nuclear submarine base on the Georgia side of St. Mary's River.

Amelia wobbled for a moment, then lost her balance and tumbled into the sea. Her paddleboard flew into the air and was caught by a crashing wave. The board slammed down, striking Amelia on the back of her head.

CHAPTER 2

The River

Amelia opened her eyes and looked around. She was in front of a high school—her high school. *What the hell? How did I get here?* she thought. *This is impossible!* The scene before her was filtered through a fine, glowing haze, like it was a hologram of her former school. It was also silent, without the expected sounds of traffic passing by or birds singing in the maple trees lining the walkway.

As if in a dream, she strode toward the front doors. Feeling a hand on her shoulder, she spun around to see a lovely young woman grinning at her. The woman was petite with flowing dark hair and a radiant smile.

"Oh my God! Linda, I haven't seen you in years. But you—you died decades ago. You were what, twenty-two or twenty-three?"

"Yes, I was twenty-three. Yet, you kept me in your thoughts, even though we didn't know each other well," answered Linda.

"You were so pretty and popular and full of life. I admired your confidence. You're right, I've thought about you many times. And you look like you did in high school! I, on the other hand, am old, wrinkled, and thick in the middle."

"Here we can choose our appearance, and look any age we want."

Amelia was shocked. "Where's here?"

"What do you think?"

"I'm—I'm on the other side? Did I die?" Amelia asked.

"Not quite. Your body is in a coma. It's your choice whether to stay on this side or return. Free will. But if you do go back, you'll be happy to know that there's little damage to your body. Your soul has chosen to stay here, at least for a while, and learn."

"I thought I'd see my parents and Michael's dad when I crossed over. I miss them, and I often feel they're around me."

"They're always near when you need them. If you decide to stay, Amelia, you'll be reunited."

"I felt bad that you died so young."

"I've always kept close to you, and you've felt my presence. We're part of the same soul group that connects in lifetimes over and over again. I've watched your triumphs and your sorrows. I've seen you raise your children. I'm glad that your marriage is so strong. I was even there on the darkest day of your life."

Amelia gasped. "Oh, my God! I felt so alone that night. Are you a guardian angel?"

"Not really," Linda answered. "More like a friend who checks in every so often. I've been busy on this side, working with children who cross over."

Amelia flopped onto a bench and tried to make sense of the situation. "So, I'm in my astral body and I agreed to come here, or at least my soul did. My physical body is in a coma in the hospital. What am I supposed to learn about?"

Linda smiled and shrugged as she settled on the bench.

"I get it," Amelia said. "I have to figure it out on my own, like Dorothy in *The Wizard of Oz*. If I've gone to the trouble of almost dying, there must be a good reason. I want to know the truth. Will this be the life review I've heard about?"

"In a way. It's important for you to not only see the past but get a deeper understanding of what you call 'truth'."

"That's interesting since I now live in a post-truth, alternative-facts society. It was more than anger and disappointment after the election; it was like an arrow went through my heart and pierced my soul. It's a spiritual, as well as intellectual and emotional wound."

"There was a profound effect on this side, too," Linda said.

"There's a mentally unstable president with malignant narcissism. I never thought tyranny would take over the country. So many of us can't even mention his name. We call him 45 or T and other less charitable things. That name will never cross my lips."

"I completely understand, Amelia."

"One bright spot is the millions of people who continue to march and take action to protest, including young people who are involved for the first time."

"The protest activity has shifted the energy of humanity. It's a primal response against authoritarianism. It's up to each individual to continue to stand up and be counted."

"You're right, Linda. Millions have supported Planned Parenthood, Muslims, and Native Americans. And the dozens of other battles that could impact the country for generations to come."

"You must keep the fire of democracy burning over the long run, which in this realm is a millisecond in time," said Linda. "It's the political and religious extremists on all sides who create the most trauma."

"I know. We can't let the radical GOP members turn back the clock seventy years on women's rights, human rights, free speech, and the care of the earth. I don't know what I personally can do about it."

Linda smiled. "Maybe you can bring some clarity to your corner of the world. Only light and love can dispel the dark. There must be a reason why you moved from Canada to the States."

Amelia sighed, shook her head, and closed her eyes. When she opened them, she and Linda were no longer in front of the high school. They were sitting on a large boulder, beside a swiftly flowing river. The scene had a dream-like quality; the water flowing over and around large rocks momentarily entranced her. A heavy rope dangled from an oak branch that reached halfway across the river. She could hear the sounds of the forest, the gurgling water and chirping birds over quietly rustling leaves.

"Amelia, do you recognize this place?"

"Of course! I spent many summer days here in the woods to get away from suburbia. We used to float down the river on inner tubes. We'd swing out on that rope and drop into the water on hot days. I loved the freedom I felt in nature. It was great."

The sound of chattering girls came from the woods. Amelia turned around and was shocked to see herself at 12 years old, walking with a group of friends. They were carrying blankets and brown paper bags. They spread out their blankets on the forest floor and took peanut butter sandwiches wrapped in wax paper and cartons of milk from the bags.

They walked to the edge of the river and inspected a large snapping turtle sunning on a rock. One of the girls went to pet it, but the reptile snapped at her hand. They laughed and left the turtle to his solitude.

"Can they see us?" said Amelia.

"No, it's like Scrooge's experience—we can see them but they can't see or hear us."

"Look how young we were! I always thought I was unattractive, but I was kind of cute. Childhood wasn't easy for me, and I was so grateful to have these friends. I was shy and insecure."

Amelia and Linda watched the girls as they giggled and talked about boys, their parents, and their siblings. The preteens lay back in the dappled sunlight pouring through the trees. A tiny white bunny hopped across Amelia's blanket, and the girls squealed with delight. It disappeared into the forest.

Right after the rabbit scurried away, a boy emerged from the underbrush and approached them. He was scrawny, with a brush cut and thick, wire-framed glasses.

"Can I join you?" he asked.

The girls bolted upright and looked at each other. Finally, 12-year-old Amelia said, "Yeah, OK, Jonah." He sat on a blanket, and Amelia handed him half of her sandwich.

"I remember that day," grown-up Amelia said. "We all thought he was weird, but I felt bad for him. Looking back, I would guess he had Asperger's—but we didn't have a name for it then. When I think of it, there was so much about mental health we didn't understand in the sixties."

"Do you want to know what he felt at that moment?" said Linda.

"Yes, I said I want to know the truth."

Amelia felt a strong vibration, then swooshed into Jonah's body. She peered through his eyes at the scene before him. She could hear his thoughts and feel his emotions. An instant later, her consciousness emerged from the boy. She gasped and took several deep breaths.

Linda touched Amelia's arm. Once again, they were sitting on the bench in front of the high school. Neither spoke for a long moment.

"What did you learn?" Linda inquired.

"Wow, that was intense! I felt waves of his emotions flow over me, and most of them were confused and painful. He really did have a difficult time understanding social norms and facial cues. The depth of his loneliness breaks my heart. He felt no one understood his reality."

"So his truth was influenced by his Asperger's syndrome, correct?" Linda asked.

"Yeah, it was. I've thought about that recently, how personality and mental disorders impact someone's view of life. Like the pathological liar who can't stop lying, or the psychopath who has no conscience. Are they capable of telling the truth? And what can happen when someone with a personality disorder gets into a position of absolute power is terrifying."

"That's the world you're living in right now. And it can be difficult to comprehend," Linda added. "There are many possible outcomes to your dire political situation."

"I'd really like to help in some way, but I'm not sure how. I've marched, signed every petition, donated to the resistance movement, and sent messages to elected officials. What else can I do?"

Linda said, "Perhaps the way will be revealed when you return."

"I hope so. Every week brings a new nightmare. Oh, do you know what happened to Jonah? His family moved away at the end of that summer."

"They moved to Toronto, and his parents found an elementary school that was able to help him deal with his Asperger's. High school was horrible for him. But he never forgot your kindness that day. Every time he was extremely upset, he'd have a peanut butter sandwich to calm himself down."

Amelia laughed. "Very cool! I had no idea I had an impact on anyone like that. He did well in school. What happened when he grew up?"

"He moved to Vancouver and became a lawyer. He's now an advocate for the Autism Speaks organization."

"It's amazing what one small act can do. Does everyone who dies and has a life review get to inhabit someone else's body and see through their eyes?" Amelia asked.

"Some do. Most simply see the events of their past. They feel the love and joy, as well as the pain and suffering that their intentional and unintentional actions created. People with great power experience every positive and negative emotion that impacted others due to their actions. This can take eons in the case of leaders who preside over the suppression or death of large groups, especially if they created unnecessary conflicts or wars."

"I guess that's what cosmic justice is all about. You reap what you sow—eventually."

"If people understand and embrace the concept that we are spiritual beings made from divine love," Linda said, "humans will be able to see with their spiritual eyes as well as their physical eyes."

"Maybe that's a better than saying 'live in the moment.' On a practical level, we have to learn from the past and think about what we need to do in the days to come."

"That's correct. The concept can be misunderstood. The president lives in the moment too much, as he's demonstrated by his tweets and undisciplined comments. He's like a child who doesn't learn from previous actions, or consider the future impact of his words. This isn't an exemplary way of being."

"You're so right," Amelia said. "We should gain knowledge from the past and incorporate the lessons into our daily decisions."

"People should also feel all their emotions—the fear, anger, frustration and even despair as well as the joy, love, and happiness. The light and shadow sides of humanity. But before you take action, in either words or deeds, open your spiritual eyes."

"I get it. We should see life through the eyes of love whether we're focused on the past, present, or future. I've always believed that our ego, or personality, is an important part of being human. Instead of trying to suppress or deny it, we need to embrace it. We are spirit, body, and mind."

"Well said, Amelia. In the coming days, you'll also have to face the traditional ways people have approached the mind-body-spirit connection. This will be in relation to organized religion."

CHAPTER 3

The Rat

Linda gently touched Amelia's arm again. They found themselves in the high school cafeteria during lunchtime. A young Amelia and her gymnastics teammates were taking their seats at a large table. Beside them was a girl named Carly. She had dark, cropped hair, and wore a ratty-looking jean jacket. A group of well-dressed fraternity boys walked by and began heckling the girl.

They mercilessly slung insults at Carly, calling her dyke and other homophobic names. Sixteen-year-old Amelia and her friends were visibly shaken, but remained silent. Finally, Carly fled the room in tears.

"You knew what they were doing was wrong, but you remained silent. Two words could have changed the situation: 'Stop it.' But you didn't have the courage to speak up," Linda said.

"I know," Amelia answered. "I was so insecure about my own social standing when I was that age, I didn't have the nerve to confront those bullies. I felt guilty about not doing anything."

"Yet there was a spark of change in you that day that you may not be aware of. Do you remember the next time you were in a similar situation, in university?"

Before Amelia could answer, she and Linda were in a bar on her university campus. The dark, smoke-filled room was packed with students dancing and drinking. A band was playing and the noise in the room was at full volume.

"We're at the Rat! The Rathskeller Pub, on campus near my dorm. I'd forgotten about this place. There was cheap beer and great music."

A group of girls walked in, including 19-year-old Amelia. They found a table and ordered glasses of beer. At a table next to them, two girls were deep in conversation with their heads almost touching. Three boys approached and began a homophobic verbal assault.

The adult Amelia watched as her young counterpart turned and assessed the situation, then stood up and stormed over.

"What's wrong with you morons? Why do you care if they're gay? Why does it matter to you?"

"Another effing lesbian! Come on guys. These broads make me sick," said one of the harassers. The young men sauntered away, laughing.

"Linda, I remember that night. I was furious, and finally had the courage to say something. So, am I going to pop into one of the girls to see their experience, like I did with Jonah?"

"No," said Linda, "you're going to see the perspective of one of the boys."

An instant later, Amelia zoomed into Peter, the tallest of the boys. She experienced Peter's inner state—she heard his thoughts and felt his emotions. With another swoosh; she was out of his body. Linda touched her arm and they were back on the high school bench.

"What did you learn about Peter's reality?" asked Linda.

"Well, it was quite a trip! I got to see flashes of *his* life pass before my eyes. He was raised as a Catholic, and his mother was a fanatic. She almost died giving birth to her sixth child. Peter accepted most of the church's teachings, including the idea that homosexuality is a sin punishable by an eternity in hell. But when he saw his mother close to death, he began to question whether the ban on any type of contraception was correct. Then he started questioning other dogma as well."

"How did this impact him?"

Amelia took a deep breath before responding. "I could feel his panic and anger toward the doctrine that almost took his mother's life. He started to become hostile toward the church teachings that didn't make sense in his adolescent mind. Babies would spend eternity in limbo if they weren't baptized? Women were supposed to have as many babies as God would give them regardless of the family circumstances? Mentally ill people would burn in hell if they committed suicide?"

"Does any of that sound familiar?"

"Why, yes! I had many of the same questions running through my mind as a teenager. That's why I left the church, especially when I found out that the priest who had married Michael and I had raped little boys then killed himself."

"Did you notice that Peter remained silent when his friends were harassing those girls?"

"I didn't. I saw them as a single unit of hate. It's interesting how we lump people together, especially in highly-charged situations. Now it makes sense. He was distraught at his friends' bullying, but didn't have the courage to stop them. I guess we each reach our tipping points where we stand up for our beliefs. Peter wasn't ready to do that."

"What else did you pick up?"

Amelia stood up and paced around the front of the school.

"His religious conditioning played havoc with his innate sense of right and wrong. He realized that fear was at the root of many teachings and that religion uses fear, guilt, and shame to control its members. He was coming to believe that biology was the reason people are gay, understanding that it was not a lifestyle choice."

"God or the Universal Power or whatever you want to call our Source is only love and doesn't sit in judgment. It's our own souls that judge the quality of our character and the actions of our lives," Linda added.

"I remember hearing the quote that religion is the opium of the masses. I think social media is the new opium of the masses," Amelia said. "It's wonderful that the world is so connected, but there's a downside to it all."

Linda stood up and approached Amelia. "Peter had that spark of change the night that you stood up for those girls. He wondered why it mattered to him, and realized other people's sexual orientation was their business, not his. You'll be happy to know that when he was in his twenties, he stopped an attack on a gay man and saved his life."

"Wow, once again a single action had a far-reaching impact on others. By the way, what ever happened to Carly?"

"Unfortunately, she couldn't take the pressure of her family's rejection and committed suicide when she was nineteen."

Amelia gasped and put her hand on her heart. Tears welled in her eyes. "If only I'd spoken up that day..."

"That's what the earth plane is all about," Linda responded. "Acknowledging our mistakes and taking measures to not repeat them. You've done well. Here, let me show you."

Linda touched Amelia's arm again and they were transported to another time and place. Amelia was thrilled to see her sons, Sasha and Ben, and her daughter Lottie sitting around the kitchen table. They were talking about their homework, school, and their lacrosse and hockey schedules. Michael walked in, dropped his suitcase, and gave them all a hug.

"Sorry I missed your game last night, Ben. How'd it go?"

"Two assists and a penalty," Ben answered.

"What happened?" Michael asked.

"I got two minutes in the sin bin for fighting."

The younger adult Amelia said, "Honey, you know I can't stand fighting in hockey, but Ben's heart was in the right place. He was defending his teammate when a player on the other team called him the n-word."

"I would have done the same thing," said Sasha. "Something like that happened at school last week. I couldn't just stand by, and ended up in a yelling match with some racist jerks. I thought we were all going to be sent to the principal's office, but Mr. Stone settled everyone down."

"Sasha! Why didn't you tell me about that?" asked young Amelia.

"Stuff like that happens all the time, Mom," Sasha answered.

"I don't understand this bullying, ignorant society. I hope common sense and compassion rule in the future," said Amelia.

"Don't count on it, Mum," added Lottie. "I've been trying to help my friend with autism for almost a decade, and he's constantly harassed."

"Well, my darlings, I still hope that society will become kinder and more empathetic."

"I do too," added Michael. "A lack of civility is never the answer."

Linda touched Amelia's arm and they were back on the bench once again. "I didn't think you needed to peer through the eyes of your family because you know them so well and understand their perspectives," Linda said.

"I was so hopeful and naïve. I truly believed this country was moving toward a spiritually enlightened society. That we would leave our children a better world."

"What did Lottie say immediately after the last election?" asked Linda. Amelia smiled. "She said that she's going to run for public office to defend the rights of women and children. And some day I know she will be a United States senator or congresswoman, and have a profound impact."

"So, what have you learned, Dorothy?"

Amelia chuckled. "Well Belinda, my good witch of the north, I learned that we have to be sensitive to other people's perspectives—to try and see through their eyes before making judgments. That existence is filtered through a person's experiences, and there are subjective realities. But I also believe that there are objective facts, and we have to stand up for what we know are empirical truths."

"And..." said Linda.

"And," Amelia began, "in each moment and with every thought and action, we have the opportunity to make the world a better place. Sometimes we see the impact, and sometimes we don't. Yet if we seek the truth, teach our children to be honest, have respect for human rights, and fight against falsehoods, then there's hope."

"Remember that. There's always hope—even when you live in a blue lies world. And beware of religious extremists and the KNC. The truth be told, Amelia."

CHAPTER 4

Dead People

M umma, wake up. I know you can hear me," said Lottie. She paced the room, taking an elastic band from her wrist to put her shoulder-length blond hair into a ponytail. The slim 26-year-old flopped into a bedside chair, then gently held her mother's hand. It had been three days since Amelia's run-in with a paddleboard had put her in a coma, and Lottie was starting to panic. Michael entered the hospital room and put his hand on his daughter's shoulder.

"Take a break, Sweetie. I can sit with your mom for a while."

"I will soon, Dad. I just *know* she can hear me. I have to bring her back!"

Tears rolled down Lottie's cheeks as she continued to stroke Amelia's hand and sob quietly. Michael, tall and well built, with salt-and-pepper hair, walked around the bed and dropped into a chair. Their sons, Sasha and Ben, came in carrying vases of flowers. Roses, balloons, and cards filled the room.

"There are so many flowers in here already. Maybe you should take some of them to the nurses' station," Michael suggested.

"No, Dad! I want the room full of flowers when Mum wakes up," said Lottie as she took out a tissue and dried her eyes.

"Dad's right," said Sasha. "It looks like a funeral parlor in here."

"*Sasha!* How can you say that?" Lottie yelled.

"I'm not saying it *is* a funeral parlor," Sasha barked back.

"Enough!" Amelia whispered. "Enough, you two."

They all turned toward the figure in the bed. Amelia's eyes fluttered, opened for a second, then closed again.

"Mumma! Open your eyes!" cried Lottie.

Michael grabbed his wife's hand. "Amelia! Can you hear me?"

Slowly, Amelia opened her eyes and looked at the worried faces around her. "What...what happened? Where am I?"

A chorus of cheers and laughter filled the room. Everyone hugged Amelia in turn. A nurse rushed into the room to see the jubilation, and quickly checked Amelia's vital signs.

"Welcome back, Mrs. Jones," said Nurse Thompson. "You're in the Amelia Island hospital. What do you remember of your accident?"

Amelia struggled to speak. The nurse poured a glass of water and brought the straw to Amelia's lips. After a few sips, Amelia looked around and smiled at her family. "I'm in the hospital? This is one way to get you all together," she said in a barely audible voice.

"We're so glad you're awake! Do you remember what happened?" asked Lottie.

"Water...I remember water all around me."

Michael helped her with the details. "You were paddleboarding with Lyla, and the board struck you on the head. She was able to pull you to shore, and a lifeguard resuscitated you. The kids flew in right away."

"You've been out of it for three days, Mom," said Ben. "We were so scared you wouldn't wake up." Suddenly, Ben started to cry.

"It's all right, Sweetie," Amelia said softly. "You can't get rid of me that easily."

Twenty-eight-year-old Sasha put his arms around his brother, who was three years younger. The boys were similar in height and build. Sasha's short, curly hair and Ben's long, straight hair were the main differences in their appearance.

Ben took a deep breath and accepted the tissue that his sister handed him.

"I guess these are tears of relief," he said. Ben gave Sasha a quick hug, then moved to the bedside and held his mother. Amelia embraced her son, then put her hand on her bandaged head. "I have a splitting headache." She tried to sit up, but fell back on the pillow.

"It's going to take some time to fully recover, Mrs. Jones," said the nurse. "But if your tests look good, you should be released in a day or two."

"Can I have some water, please?" said Amelia. After a few sips, she quietly spoke. "I do remember paddleboarding with Lyla. There was a pod of beautiful dolphins. Then what? Oh, the storm was coming in, and we were trying to get to shore. Something startled me."

Michael added, "Lyla said two Navy helicopters roared overhead, and you lost your balance. The board was caught in a wave and hit you in the head."

"I guess it will slowly come back to me."

Michael took a cloth from the side table and carefully dotted the beads of perspiration from his wife's forehead. He gently kissed her cheek.

Amelia smiled at her husband, then looked at her children. "So, my darlings, I hope you can stay until I get out of here. We need to celebrate my return from the other side."

"Do you remember anything?" asked Sasha. "Did you have an NDE, a near-death experience? Did you see a tunnel and bright light? Were you in a beautiful landscape? Did your life flash before your eyes?"

Amelia placed her hand on her head. "My mind is still fuzzy—I'm not sure. Oh, wait! Linda, a girl I knew in high school was there. That's right; we were standing in front of the school. But she died decades ago, so I knew something wasn't right."

"So, you talk to dead people?" Sasha added with a grin.

Amelia laughed, then started to cough. Lottie held the glass of water to her mother's lips, and she drank until she regained her breath.

"Go on, honey," said Michael.

"I feel like what Linda and I talked about is on the tip of my tongue. I don't know. It was something really important, but..."

"It's OK, Mumma," Lottie said. "Take your time trying to remember. We'll all stay until you get out of the hospital, won't we, boys?"

"You bet," said Ben.

"We're here for you, Mom," added Sasha.

"I'll stay with your mother. You three can go back to the house and get some rest. This strong lady isn't leaving us any time soon."

"Come on, bros," said Lottie. "You both need a shower."

CHAPTER 5

Auras

The morning sun poured over Amelia as she sat on her back patio. Mallard ducks and Canada geese paddled around the pond behind the house. Sasha, Lottie, and Ben walked out with steaming mugs of coffee and sat in the chairs around their mother. They all remained silent for a long while.

"Too bad that dad had to leave for his meeting. I'm glad we're able to hang here for a few days. Things are slow at work this week," said Lottie.

"I caught up on work this morning, but it's a good week for me to be away too," added Ben.

"I'm sorry it took a paddleboard to the head to get us all together, but I'm so glad you're here, my wonderful children."

"We are too, Mom! Do you remember anything else?" asked Sasha. "I've read a lot about NDE's, near-death experiences and ADE's, or actual-death experiences. Sometimes people come back and have healing abilities, or precognition."

Amelia laughed. "I don't think I have either of those, but I have been getting flashes of images from my time on the other side. I didn't see God or go to a magical land. After Linda and I were at the high school, we went back to when I was twelve. I was at the river with some friends, and a boy with Asperger's joined us. For just a moment, I went into his body was able to see through his eyes and understand what he was feeling."

"Wow," said Ben, "that's crazy! Like in the movie *Ghost*, where those spirits take over Whoopi Goldberg's body. I'd like to be able to do that in real life."

Lottie asked, "What did you learn?"

Amelia rose from her chair and walked to the edge of the pond. She turned toward her children, and saw soft colors swirling around their heads. She gasped. Her heart was pounding and her head was spinning.

"Mom, what's wrong?" said Ben.

"Oh my gosh! I can see your auras! There are colors emanating from your heads and shoulders. There's a glowing white light around you, with swirling shades of blue, green, gold, and purple. I've read about auras, but I've never seen them before!"

"Cool! Are they the same for all of us?" asked Sasha.

"Similar, but some colors are stronger for each of you. Amazing! Oh, now they're fading. That was incredible." Amelia walked back and flopped into the chair.

"I'm not sure why that happened."

Sasha held his mother's hand. "Mom, I think you might have more psychic powers since your accident. Do you feel different?"

"In a way," Amelia began. "I'm not afraid of death, although I really wasn't afraid before. I know without a doubt that our consciousness survives the body. And we are definitely spiritual beings, having a human experience. But I'm not sure about paranormal capabilities coming out."

"Back to what happened when you were twelve, what did you learn when you zipped into the boy's body?" Lottie inquired.

"It was all about truth—subjective truth. When we were kids, we hadn't heard of Asperger's or autism. I could see from his perspective that he didn't have the ability to read people's facial expressions and gauge their reactions to his words. He suffered a lot. I was pleased to learn from Linda that my welcoming him that summer day had a profound impact on his life. I shared my peanut butter sandwich with him, and that became his go-to way to deal with stressful situations."

"So, we all filter the truth through our personal experiences?" Sasha asked.

"Yes. Maybe I had that experience because I've been questioning the nature of truth. Ever since the pathological liars have taken over the White

House, I've been in a state of anxiety. I try not to let it bother me, but every new revelation of the attempted dictatorship infuriates me."

"Me too, Mom," Ben and Sasha said together. They all laughed and it lightened the mood considerably.

"So even though there's a subjective truth for each of us, we can't ignore objective reality. Facts like the sun rises in the east and sets in the west, and climate change is real, are empirical facts," added Amelia. "And when we inevitably make a mistake, we have to own it and make corrections."

"That's something the GOP won't do; they just double down on their lies and blame others," said Ben. "Sasha, your sign at the January 21st march was great: 'men of quality respect women's equality.'"

"It was so cool that all of us marched that day, including dad," said Lottie.

"Mom, your spirituality group will want to know about your NDE."

"You're right, Ben. We have a FaceTime meeting next week. I'm glad that Lyla has joined the group. I hope I remember more about the other side before the meeting."

Sasha, Lottie, and Ben were each lost in thought, digesting what Amelia had said. The future belonged to their generation, and they were the ones who had to ensure their country didn't get submerged in a sea of lies.

"Mom, do you think the Russia thing will bring him down?" Ben asked.

"I'm not sure. There are other countries working on his ties through the businesses he and his family run. They've suggested money laundering by Russian oligarchs and mafia that can be directly tied to 45. I hope they can uncover enough to impeach him on treason or the emoluments clause, or force him to resign like Nixon."

Sasha added, "They talked about pay for play with Clinton, and yet the disgusting son-in-law's sister was openly selling US visas to rich Chinese! The Republicans are so corrupt they won't take any action against this tyranny."

Ben got up from is chair and was heading inside when he stopped short.

"Guys, look across the pond. There's a man with a huge camera taking pictures of us!"

Everyone turned toward the house across the water and saw a figure duck behind the home.

"Yeah, I saw him," said Sasha. "That was a major zoom lens, like the ones they use at football games. Why the hell was he taking photos of us?"

"That's so creepy!" Lottie added. "There's no way he was just taking pictures of the neighborhood."

"But why us?" Ben asked.

CHAPTER 6

A True Knight

F ather Henry Rathbone had known since childhood that he would be a priest. His brother Ted was ten years older, and had openly rebelled against the Catholic Church. This broke his mother's heart; Henry vowed to make amends for his only sibling's betrayal.

His dad had been emotionally cold with a volatile temper. Both boys had been beaten with a strap repeatedly for minor offenses. When he was 18, Ted confronted his father and stopped the beatings. Mr. Rathbone deserted the family shortly after. Henry was both devastated and relieved. The traumatic event created a split in his personality at the tender age of 8. As an adult, Henry still compartmentalized his life: a devout priest by day, and one who broke his vows at night with his young mistress.

Henry was fascinated by the history of the Knights Templar and their defense of the Catholic Church. When he took his final vows as a priest, he knew he'd defend the 21st century church with the same intensity. He had the valiant heart of a true soldier, and would fight for his religion.

He hadn't expected to challenge the leader of his church, but the new pope was endangering the traditional dogma and teachings. It was shortly after the pope was elected that Henry joined Opus Dei, the fanatical wing of Catholicism. He wasn't involved in self-flagellation, though; he'd had quite enough beatings as a child.

CHAPTER 7

The Witch

A melia and Lottie drove into the quaint Victorian town of Fernandina Beach. They traveled down the curving, tree-lined street past historic buildings, eclectic shops, and a variety of restaurants. They parked in front of the pirate statue guarding the Palace Saloon, Florida's oldest continuous bar. Strolling to the harbor in the warm sunlight, Amelia's mood brightened. Nighttime dreams and flashes of daytime visions had been haunting her since the accident.

"It's funny that you moved to an island with your name," Lottie commented. "It's a cool place, with great beaches. I love the ancient oak trees dripping with Spanish moss. It's so different from the other parts of Florida."

"There's nowhere else I'd rather live. I feel inspired by the number of artists and writers in town. Maybe I'll become a painter or a novelist. Who knows?"

They entered a restaurant by the wharf and were quickly seated at an outdoor table. Huge brown pelicans swooped over the sailboats gently bobbing in the water. They could see the pale marshlands and the state of Georgia across the river. After ordering, Amelia closed her eyes and inadvertently went into a light trance. A moment later she jerked forward, startling her daughter.

"Mumma! Are you OK?"

"Whoa! What a weird vision. I wonder how long this will keep happening. That board sure messed with my brain."

"What was your vision about?"

"I was walking in front of the White House and an overwhelming wave of fear engulfed me. Then I was grabbed and thrown into a white van."

"Oh, Mum! That must have brought back terrible memories," Lottie said.

"It...it did. I still have nightmares about that horrible time. I wake up screaming and scare the heck out of your dad."

"You're not planning a trip to Washington, are you?"

"I've no plans to go anywhere. When your dad gets home from his business trip, we're looking forward to staying put and enjoying the new house."

Lottie said, "I want you to feel safe even when Dad's gone. Always remember to activate the alarm when you're alone."

Amelia wanted to change the subject. "I know I was joking earlier, but maybe I will try my hand at writing. A resistance novel would be interesting—or maybe a persistence novel. I've been volunteering for so long I think it's time to try something new."

"Good idea. I'm thinking about how I can incorporate what's happening into the education policy I'm working on. There's a completely incompetent person in charge of education, and now they want to destroy the department. That way they can deny evolution and teach creationism, and say the Holocaust wasn't about the annihilation of Jews. Also, that the Civil War wasn't about slavery but was a 'War of Northern Aggression' based on economics and state's rights. Insane!"

"How can we have devolved so quickly?" Amelia asked.

"It's crazy that my daughter, when I have her, may have to fight for the basic women's rights that her grandmother and great grandmother fought for. That's not progress," said Lottie. "I guess I'd better find a boyfriend before I talk about having a baby."

"It's a spiritually juvenile society that's now evident to all who care to see. I want that to change before my grandchildren arrive."

"There's lots of time for that, Mumma!"

"Even so, the underbelly of the alt-right has been exposed, and it's not pretty. All the sludge has risen to the surface: misogyny, anti-Semitism, homophobia, xenophobia, and racism. It's like we're living in a reality show hosted by a demented pervert. A Jerry Springer-like world gone mad, and an administration full of disgraceful enablers."

"I know," Lottie agreed. "But I still have faith in the basic goodness of most people."

"You're right, Sweetie. Millions of people, women and men of all ages and ethnicities, continue to stand up and demand to be heard. It's terrible how undocumented immigrants have been terrorized and families torn apart. We'll fight the good fight for as long as it takes."

Amelia added, "It's distressing that we're not just fighting diplomatic battles. The missiles in Syria and massive bomb in Afghanistan are horrendous. Where will this all lead? How many people will die under this group of war mongers?"

Lottie and Amelia finished lunch and headed to the car. They drove down the beach road past old-fashioned beach cottages, condos, and new mini-mansions. They pulled into the doctor's office next to the hospital. Exiting the car, they encountered Nurse Thompson, walking briskly toward them. Amelia went to hug the nurse, who pulled back dramatically. The shock on Amelia's face was evident.

"Hi, I want to thank you for helping my mom," said Lottie.

"I wanted to thank you, too," Amelia added. "Are you OK?"

Nurse Thompson hurried toward her car and pressed the remote to unlock the vehicle. "Yes, I'm fine. Glad you're better. I have to go," the nurse called over her shoulder. She got into her car, slammed the door, and sped out of the parking lot.

"Well, *that* was weird. What's her problem?" Lottie asked.

"I don't know." Amelia leaned against the car to steady herself. "Wait—now I remember. After you all left on the night I woke up, the nurse came in and was taking my pulse. I asked her how long she had worked at the hospital. I felt this strong vibration go through my body. Then, without warning, she let out a tirade against the doctor who was on call that night, and the head nurse."

"Wow," said Lottie. "That's strange. No wonder she freaked when she saw you. She's probably worried that you're going to tell hospital administration what she said. You could cause her a lot of trouble. What did you say?"

"Nothing, she rushed out of the room. Oh, my God! I just thought of something else. The doctor came in a while later. When he was checking my head wound, I asked him how he was doing. That strange energy went through me again. Then, he told me that he'd been taking extra shifts lately, since his wife found out about his affair with a nurse."

"*What?*" said Lottie. "What did you say to him?"

"Once again, he put my bandage back on and ran out of the room. Another memory just came back. I heard them talking outside my door later that night. The nurse said something about the witch in the room made her confide something she didn't want anyone to know. The doctor told her the same thing had happened to him!"

Lottie and Amelia began walking to the doctor's office, silently mulling over what had occurred with the nurse and doctor in the hospital.

"It seems that both of them told you something when they were touching you. Physical contact with you may have prompted their confessions. But Dad, the boys, and I have touched you many times, and it hasn't happened to us."

Their conversation was interrupted when a tall, striking, black woman approached. She gave Amelia a bear hug and laughed heartily.

"My, oh my, Amelia!" said Ruby Lewis. "I'm so thrilled you're doing better. You look darn good for someone just out of a coma."

"Ruby! It's great to see you too. You must be glad you didn't come paddleboarding with us. Lyla is still recovering from having to drag me to shore. I gave her a terrible fright. You remember my daughter, Lottie?"

Ruby bear-hugged Lottie as well. "Of course I do, Sugar. You're prettier than ever, Lottie. How's that big job of yours going?"

Lottie was happy to be released and grinned at her mother's friend. "The job's great, thanks for asking. I've always wanted to help children, and I'm in the perfect position for that."

"So how are you, Amelia? Are you OK?"

"Except for a few strange side effects, I'm recovering nicely. I'm heading in to see Dr. Ward right now so he can check on my head wound. How have you been?"

Ruby held Amelia's arm. "Pretty good. I'll be at my sister's for a few days. She's leaving her abusive, alcoholic husband, and we're planning her escape. Oh, heavens! I shouldn't have said that. No one is supposed to know!"

"Don't worry, your secret's safe with us," said Amelia.

"Oh, good, good. I've got to go. Call me."

Ruby walked away quickly, with a troubled look on her face. Amelia and Lottie continued into the doctor's office. Amelia signed in and they sat in the waiting room.

"You seem to be scaring people away, Mum."

Amelia chuckled nervously. "They tell me intimate details, then rush away. Very strange."

"So, they touch you, spill their guts, then bolt. You're going to have to keep testing this newfound ability of yours. Try it on Dr. Ward when he checks your head. Ask him a question about something personal and see what he says. I wish I could go in with you to see the expression on his face if it's something juicy."

"Lottie! I don't want to know anyone's private thoughts or secrets."

The receptionist called Amelia's name and she was ushered into an examination room. A young nurse took her temperature, blood pressure, and pulse. The nurse was shy and quiet, and Amelia was glad there was very little conversation. After 10 minutes, Dr. Ward entered carrying a folder. He quickly reviewed the paperwork, then greeted Amelia.

"It's good to see you up and around. How are you feeling?"

"For the most part I'm doing well. I still get occasional headaches, but they're not too bad," answered Amelia.

"Fine, fine. Now let's take a look at that head of yours."

Amelia pulled back for a moment. She was fearful the doctor would touch her and unintentionally reveal something that was on his mind.

"It's all right, Amelia. I won't hurt you." Dr. Ward gently pulled back the bandage and gently poked around the wound.

"How does it look?" Amelia asked as her body began to vibrate.

"You're healing nicely. But people your age shouldn't be venturing out in the ocean on paddleboards when they obviously have no idea what they're doing." The doctor stepped back immediately.

"Sorry, I shouldn't have said that. I don't know what came over me!"

I do, thought Amelia. *Just touching me makes you tell me what's on your mind. And I keep getting these strange vibrations. What the hell's going on?*

Dr. Ward put on a clean bandage and quickly left the room. Amelia took a deep breath, gathered her purse, and slowly walked out.

CHAPTER 8

Swamp Monsters

On the drive home, Amelia was silent. She didn't want to alarm her daughter, but she really needed to talk to someone about what was happening to her. Before she could decide what to do, Lottie questioned her.

"Dr. Ward confessed something to you, didn't he?"

"Yes. It was fine with the nurse, but she barely said a word and I didn't ask her any questions. But with the doctor..."

"You're scaring me, Mum! What did he say? Is there something wrong with you?"

"Oh, sorry, Darling. I'm fine." Amelia giggled. "He just said that people my age shouldn't go paddleboarding in the ocean when they don't know what they're doing."

Lottie and Amelia started to laugh and couldn't stop. They pulled into the driveway and opened the garage door with the remote. They were still giggling when they went to the fridge for bottles of water.

"I think I agree with him; you should paddle in a nice, calm pond next time," said Lottie. "But what an odd thing to say."

"Everything is odd these days," Amelia complained, shaking her head. "I don't know what to make of any of this."

They took their drinks out to the lanai and gazed at the ripples in the pond. A dozen geese came swooping in, their landing gear down. The large birds glided onto the water and squawked at one another.

"Sometimes I want to scream at the insanity of this political nightmare, and other times I feel like crying. I've spent my whole adult life searching for a spirituality that will make sense of this world. Positive thinking, the Law of Attraction, our thoughts create our reality, mindfulness, karma, living in the moment. But what happens when no matter what you think or believe, you're swept into an authoritarian society?" asked Amelia.

Lottie was quiet, trying to determine the best response to her mother's question. It had been a heart-wrenching time for millions of people, especially when their protests were ineffective in stopping toxic appointees to the Cabinet and Supreme Court. So many basic rights people had been fighting for generation after generation had been destroyed in a matter of months. The swamp in DC had more millionaire monsters slithering around in the putrid water than ever before.

"There have been tyrants and dictators throughout human history. I honestly didn't think it would happen here," Lottie began. "Barbarians in the White House... The very foundation of our democracy has been undermined. What's next?"

"I don't know, Sweetheart. I have to admit that no amount of positive thinking or living in the moment will solve our problems. Although I still believe that meditation and mindfulness are important."

"You're right, Mumma. There has to be a balance between our spiritual practices and physical action."

"We need to examine the past and *learn* from it. The Holocaust wasn't that long ago, but people have forgotten what fascism looks like. And too many people simply don't care unless it affects them personally. Take away their healthcare and they're mad as hell; take away someone else's care and they don't give a damn. Build the wall but don't take my land for it."

"The constant lies make me sick—with or without healthcare! And even if he's impeached or resigns, all his appointees have damaged the country and the whole world for years to come," said Lottie.

"If only the truth be told," said Amelia. "Wait! That's the last thing Linda said to me before I came back. I still don't remember a lot of the details, but I know it was important for me to recall that concept."

"The truth be told," mused Lottie. "I like that."

"I don't like to use the word hate, so I'll say I detest what's become of this country. We have to get back to the concept of facts being facts. We need truth and transparency more than ever."

"That's what you can write about, Mum: how so many people are traumatized by the election. I'm going to miss our conversations when I leave tomorrow."

"Me too, my sweet angel. Hmm, the truth be told. And the letters KNC just popped into my head."

"I've never heard of the KNC," Lottie added. "Is it a political group?"

"I'm not sure. I'll have to look it up on the internet."

The following morning, Lottie flew back to her home in San Francisco. Amelia was alone for the next few days, until Michael returned. She was grateful that they'd found this little piece of paradise in Florida. The 13 miles of white sand beaches, the canopy roads of ancient, moss-covered oaks, and the calming pace of island life suited her well. At this point, she had no interest in big city living. Visiting Lottie in San Francisco, Sasha in Philadelphia, and Ben in Boston was enough of the big city lights.

Amelia sat at her kitchen table and opened her laptop to confirm the time and date of her next spirituality group meeting. The Sassy Seekers had been together for three years. Amelia connected with them online since her move from Boston. *I think Lyla will get along well with the women in this group,* thought Amelia. *There's going to be a lot to talk about at the next meeting.*

She typed *KNC* into the search engine, but there were no relevant matches. The mystery remained. Then the thought of religious zealots popped into her mind and she began a new search. The Catholic group Opus Dei popped up and she read several entries about the fringe organization.

After turning off the computer, she found a journal, grabbed a pen, and settled into a chair on the front porch. She wrote the words *the truth be told* on the first page. "OK," she said to the palm trees swaying in the wind, "what else happened on the other side?"

Amelia put the pen on the paper and let a stream of consciousness guide her hand. An hour later, she stopped and read what she had written. Her encounters with the past—in high school, college, and with her teenage children—were all revealed. She read it over and over again, jotting down ideas that came to mind.

A car pulled into the driveway. Lyla got out with a bottle of prosecco and a box of Godiva chocolates. She was tall and lithe, with short auburn hair and a winsome smile.

"You read my mind!" said Amelia. "I just remembered what happened during my NDE. A glass of wine is exactly what I need."

"That's what friends are for," answered Lyla.

The women went into the two-story, Lowcountry-style house and popped the cork on the bottle. They took the wine and candy into the living room and enjoyed the grownup treats.

"I love the twelve-foot ceilings in this house. The layout is perfect. But most of all, I'm glad that you're settling here for good," said Lyla. "You've become a dear friend in a short time."

"You too. I'd thought about moving back to Canada, but the kids have their lives in the States, and I want to be here for them. I've decided to stand up to the administration from within the country. And I really don't like cold winters."

"That's why I left Pittsburg. I'm glad you're feeling better. You gave me quite a fright."

"Once again, Lyla, thank you for saving my life!"

"I'm just your everyday superhero. Seriously, it was fortunate that the lifeguard was there, and that she was able to resuscitate you. I won't be using a paddleboard for a very long time."

"You know it! Even my doctor said someone my age shouldn't go paddleboarding in the ocean."

"That's strange. I'm surprised he'd say that to you."

Amelia took a sip of wine. She was deciding whether to share her unusual experiences with her friend.

"That's only one of the strange things that have happened since my accident. I'll start at the beginning..."

CHAPTER 9

Crazy

Michael and Amelia were seated at their favorite Italian restaurant in Fernandina Beach. The server brought their menus, and the owner greeted them warmly. He chatted amiably while he handed them glasses of red wine. It hadn't taken long for the Joneses to feel at home on the island.

"It's great that you can work out of the house when you aren't traveling," said Amelia.

"And winning that lottery didn't hurt, even though it wasn't the big prize."

"I always knew we'd win something; I just wasn't sure when. I'm glad it finally happened, and the kids are, too. Now they have down payments for houses when they get to that point. And we're all set for retirement."

They ordered dinner and enjoyed the Chianti. "Every morning I wake up and I'm grateful that we live here. It really feels like it'll be the best place for us long term," Amelia commented.

"Florida—heaven's waiting room," Michael said. They both laughed.

"Glad we're not that old yet!" Amelia added.

"I hope we can convince one of the kids to move down here when we have grandbabies."

A young couple at the next table was engaged in a heated argument. Their voices were low, but the tension was palpable. Suddenly, the woman got up from the table and stormed out of the restaurant. Every patron and server watched her go.

"Wow, another relationship in trouble over politics," whispered Amelia. "I heard them arguing about what's happened since the election."

"People should keep calm and move on," answered Michael. "You'll make yourself nuts following every little tweet and post."

"Actually, I've been thinking of writing a novel about our troubled times. It might be the best way for me to channel my angst and make my voice heard."

"Just be careful, Amelia. There are a lot of crazy, dangerous people out there."

"Sometimes I think I'm one of the crazies. It seems I have a new ability since my accident. Several times, with people I know and some I don't, I've been able to make them say exactly what's on their minds. They touch me and reveal things they don't want to reveal. It happened with the nurse and doctor when I woke up from the coma."

"I don't understand," said Michael.

"Well, after I asked a question, there was a buzzing in my ears and a distinct vibration through my body. The nurse and doctor seemed to sense this strange frequency before they told the truth."

The server brought their dinner, and Michael began playing with his pasta. "Honey, that worries me. Are you sure it's really happening?"

Amelia became defensive. "*Of course* I'm sure. Lottie was with me once when it happened." They silently began eating. She picked at her meal.

"I didn't ask for this, but it's real. It doesn't work with you or the kids. I guess it's like a psychic who can't read her own future, or anyone's close to her."

"I hope no one outside of the family finds out about this," said Michael.

"Too late. It might be a topic of conversation at the hospital, because the nurse I mentioned freaked out when she saw me yesterday. I know she talked to the doctor who was working that night, and there was also an orderly in my room. He heard them talk about it too."

"Just be careful, Honey, please," Michael pleaded.

"I'll make sure I don't question anyone when they're touching me."

The following day, Michael left for a business trip to Arizona and Amelia tackled the garage. It was overflowing with unpacked boxes. A neighbor came by with her two young girls on bikes. Amelia waved and

Hailey walked up the driveway, her daughters trailing behind her. All three had their long, dark hair pulled back in ponytails.

"Hi, Amelia. It's looks like you're getting settled. How do you like living on the island?"

"Hello, Hailey. Hi, girls. Things are going well. I had a run-in with a paddleboard, but I'm fine now. Just a small bandage as a reminder."

"Oh my gosh! I'm glad you're OK."

"Have you lived here long?"

"About a year. We moved from Iowa. There are some things I miss, like the hayrides, fall fairs, and corn mazes," Hailey said. "But not the cold winters!"

"I won't miss the Boston winters. But I'm not fond of corn fields and farms either," Amelia said.

Hailey grabbed her youngest before she knocked over a lamp with her bike.

"Are you going to the zoning meeting for the land next to the subdivision?" Hailey asked.

"I hadn't heard of it. I guess I should start paying attention to the politics of the island. When's the meeting?"

"Tomorrow night at seven. I can pick you up if you'd like to go."

Amelia pondered for a moment. "Yes, I'd like to go. Thanks."

"I'd better get lunch for these two. I'll see you at six forty-five tomorrow."

CHAPTER 10

RV Park

T he city hall meeting room was packed with citizens concerned about the rezoning of a heavily forested area for residential use. Amelia and Hailey found seats on the aisle near the back of the room, and listened to contentious conversations all around them. A petite, redheaded woman sat down beside Hailey.

"Sandra," said Hailey, "it's good to see you. Have you met Amelia? She just moved in across the pond from you."

"No, we haven't met, but my nephew mentioned that the lady who was in a coma lived the neighborhood. He's an orderly at the hospital and lives with me. And since I know everyone else, I assumed it was the person in the blue house."

"That's me, Sandra. We're happy to be in our home. We've rented houses on the island for the last four years. We've decided this is where we want to live when my husband retires," Amelia explained.

The meeting was called to order. The participants began to state their cases for and against the planned subdivision. A young man seated behind Hailey was recording the session with a small video camera.

"This is getting heated," Hailey whispered. "Both sides have valid points, but something doesn't feel right about what the developer is saying."

"I agree," answered Amelia. "He's saying they're planning on only single-family homes, but I don't believe him. Can he change it in the future?"

"With the right support from the local government, I think he can."

The discussion went on for the next half hour, becoming more combative as the developer, Ronald Banner, tried to convince the participants that his proposal was in the best interests of the island. Opponents raised concerns and referenced his checkered history in other Florida communities. In the past, he'd forced through changes to the zoning after an initial approval to allow single-family homes. He was able to alter zoning to allow RV parks in some areas.

"I can guarantee, one hundred percent, that this will be a single-family home community," stated Mr. Banner. "Believe me."

Amelia could feel her anxiety rise. She knew in her heart that the developer couldn't be trusted. She began to see a muddy, brown energy swirling around his head. It was the second time she'd been able to see someone's aura, and this time it was disturbing. There was a buzzing in her ears and the familiar vibration in her body. She was inspired to say out loud, "The truth be told. Mr. Banner, the truth be told."

All eyes turned toward Amelia. She blushed and looked down at her hands, clutching the purse in her lap tightly. Banner's eyes darted around the room. It was like he'd received an unexpected and unwanted jolt of electricity. He shuddered, then clenched his fists, but was compelled to speak.

"I...I can assure you that I will not—or probably won't—or actually, I *do* intend to force local commissioners to rezone for RVs, and trailers for seasonal workers, on this property," said Banner.

The audience gasped at this confession, and conversations erupted throughout the room. Banner dashed out a side door. The young man seated behind Hailey captured the entire event on his camera. Amelia jumped up and ran out of the room. Hailey quickly followed her to the car, and they drove out of the parking lot. Without saying anything to Amelia, Hailey pulled into a local bar and parked.

"I think a drink is in order. And you can tell me what just happened," said Hailey.

Amelia smiled at her neighbor and got out of the car. They went into the bar and sat at a quiet table in the corner. The server took their order.

"So, I guess you want the truth, the whole truth, and nothing but the truth," said Amelia. The women started to laugh as the server placed their drinks on the table. Amelia took a big gulp of Pinot grigio.

"Absolutely!" answered Hailey. "How did you make Banner spill?"

"Well, when I was in the coma, I had what they call a near-death experience, and I actually went to the spirit world."

"My God! I didn't know. I've heard of NDEs, but haven't met anyone who's had one. How does that relate to what went down tonight?"

Amelia took another sip of wine. "I—or my consciousness, or astral body, or whatever—went to the other side. I found myself in front of my old high school, and I met a friend who passed away decades ago. She helped me see events from my past and the effect my actions have had on other people."

"Like a life review?" asked Hailey.

"In a way, except that I actually zoomed into a couple of people to see things from their perspective. It was all about subjective and objective truth. Since the coma, I've been able to see auras, or the energy field around the body. But the crazy thing is that when some people touch me and I ask a question, they blurt out the truth. I get this crazy vibration in my body that they pick up on. They had no intention of saying what was on their minds."

"But you didn't touch Banner."

"I know! That's what freaked me out. I felt strange vibrations in my body; I hadn't intended to say out loud what I was thinking, but I was compelled to do so. And I had no idea that Banner would actually tell the truth."

The women silently sipped their wine. "Hailey, do you think anyone will post what happened on the internet? I noticed a person on the far side of the room videotaping the meeting."

"If Banner can help it, he'll make sure the video won't be released. Or it will be edited to leave out the end of the meeting."

"I certainly hope you're right. I don't want anyone to know about my unusual abilities. I'll bet that people won't realize it was me who made Banner confess."

"Do you want to try it with me? I'll think of something I wouldn't normally reveal and you can ask me to tell the truth."

Amelia sighed; she didn't want to play this game. Having this ability could be frightening. Finally, she acquiesced.

"OK, let's do it. I should know what the possibilities are with this—whatever this is."

Hailey thought for a few minutes while Amelia looked around to make sure no one was listening. The vibration flowed through her body.

"I'm ready," said Hailey.

"Hailey, the truth be told."

Hailey hesitated and placed her hand over her mouth. After a moment she lowered her hand and said, "I don't want my in-laws staying with us for a month this summer. They're too nosey and interfering, especially with the girls."

The women started to laugh. "So if I meet your in-laws this summer..."

"Yeah, you'll know how I feel! That's crazy. I was determined not to say anything, but I couldn't help myself. There's something paranormal going on here."

"Sasha was saying that sometimes people come back from the other side with new talents, like healing or precognition. I suppose this is my gift!"

"So, do you share this gift or keep it to yourself?" asked Hailey.

CHAPTER 11

Precious Gems

M ichael and Amelia set up beach chairs and a bright yellow umbrella on the sparsely populated beach at the south end of the island. Michael turned his face toward a cloudless, deep blue sky and sighed. "This is a perfect Sunday! Beachside with the *New York Times* and my honey."

Amelia smiled, then handed her husband a sandwich and bottled water. "There's no place like home. Wow, that just reminded me of something that happened during my NDE. I was talking to Linda about the nature of truth, and the fact that I had to figure things out for myself, like Dorothy, before I could return home. I've always tried to be honest and instill honesty in the kids. I think we've done a good job raising them."

"They're amazing kids: the hope of a better future. Even with all the turmoil in this country, I'm confident that common sense and compassion will eventually prevail."

"I wish I was as optimistic as you are. But you're right; we should have faith that we and the next generation will stand against oppression."

"Look! There's a Navy ship on the horizon. I wonder if you can tour the Mayport Navy Yard. It's not too far south of here. I'd like to do that, if it's possible. And it's intriguing that King's Bay submarine base is near us, too. Having all those nuclear subs so close is either comforting or scary. Not sure which."

"I heard on the news that Russian spy ships are often in the area because of the sub base. Recently the ship SSV-175 Viktor Leonov was spotted off our shore. That's kind of scary. And I have no idea why that bit of information is stuck in my brain."

"A guy at the grocery store said that at King's Bay there are sea lions trained to detect scuba divers that come too close to the base."

Two Navy helicopters came roaring overhead, making Amelia jump. "I wonder if helicopters will always startle me! It's interesting that several retired admirals live in the Shipwreck Harbor neighborhood, just over the bridge."

"It's a nice community, but I'm glad we found a house on the island. It's much more convenient, and will continue to be as the area becomes more crowded."

Two children in colorful swimsuits came running over to Amelia. Their grandmother, Ruby, followed them.

"Hi, you two. What have you been up to?" asked Amelia.

"Grandma Ruby took us to the movies," said six-year-old Opal.

"And we got frozen yogurt," added big sister Pearl. "Now Grandma wants us to get some exercise. She's trying to tire us out until Mom and Dad get home."

"Hello, Amelia. Hi, Michael. These kids are smart, as well as being full of energy. Their parents are in Jacksonville for the day. I do love spending time with them."

"I can hardly wait to have grandbabies," said Amelia. "Patience isn't my best virtue, but I need to let our kids live their own lives."

Michael added, "I want them to get started soon! I need grandchildren before I'm too old to enjoy them."

Pearl and Opal kicked off their sandals and ran into the warm water. They body surfed in the rising waves. Michael stood up and offered his chair to Ruby.

"Have a seat, Ruby. I'm going for a walk and let you ladies catch up." Michael strolled south on the wide, firm beach.

Ruby lowered herself into the chair and accepted a bottle of water from Amelia. She watched her grandchildren playing in the ocean, and waved back when they called to her.

"My little precious gems. Oh, did you hear about another march on the island next month?" Ruby asked. "There are so many causes being included in these protests it's hard to keep track."

"I know. So many of our basic rights have been attacked, and every government agency has been undermined. There are protests for the environment, climate change, abortion rights, LGBT rights, immigration, refugees, equal pay, and so many others."

"And for those of us who've faced compound discrimination, it's a call to action."

"I'm not following," said Amelia.

"It's compound discrimination because I'm a woman *and* I'm black; if I was a Muslim, that would be a triple hit."

"It would be quadruple, if you were gay, too."

"I just pray that this younger generation can drag the country into the 21st century and put the *Mad Men* days in the rearview mirror. Too much regressive legislation has been passed, making the rich richer and shafting the rest of us. It may take decades to undo all the harm that's been done."

"I totally agree, Ruby. It's horrible that many people still don't care. Daily scandals and rampant incompetence are not how a government should be run."

"Mercy, it is embarrassing when I talk to my relatives in other countries. They can't understand how this could have happened."

Amelia sighed. "I get the same reaction from my family in Canada. They keep asking me when I'm going to move back. But our children have their lives here, and I love my new home. It's not that easy."

"I do understand your dilemma, Amelia. But I wish there was more accountability. And now they want to destroy the EPA! What is going on?"

"You reap what you sow, eventually."

"I'm not sure I'll live long enough to see the Republicans get their comeuppance. Can't anyone make these politicians speak the truth?"

The women watched the girls playing in the warm ocean, thinking. They sat quietly as clouds swept across the sun and changed the mood of the afternoon.

"My sister's staying with me for a while. Lord knows why it took her so long to leave that monster. Battered wife syndrome, I guess," Ruby eventually said.

"I'm glad she's finally safe. Spousal abuse is horrible. A person's self-esteem gets so tattered they can't see the reality of the situation," lamented Amelia.

"Or their fear of being physically hurt blinds them to the truth," Ruby countered.

CHAPTER 12

Famous

The following week, something unexpected came into Amelia's life. Sasha called her Monday morning, and informed her that she was becoming famous. A YouTube video was getting hundreds of shares, and his mother was the star.

"Sasha, what are you talking about?"

"Someone recorded that meeting on the new subdivision you went to. He filmed you saying, 'the truth be told,' and Banner blurting out the truth," Sasha said. "It looks like you made him be honest, even though he didn't want to be."

"Good heavens. Was my name mentioned?"

"Yeah, the guy who took the video identified you and said that you live on the island."

Amelia was in shock. "I wonder how he got my name... This is not good."

"I'm not sure, Mom. Probably someone in the room recognized you."

"How did you find out about the video?" Amelia asked.

"A guy at work saw it over the weekend, and asked me if my parents lived on Amelia Island. When I said yes, he sent me the link."

"Thanks for letting me know. Talk to you later, Love."

Amelia poured herself another cup of coffee and walked out onto the lanai. She watched the ducks popping their heads into the water, trying to catch their breakfast. The royal palms swayed gently in the breeze as massive white clouds drifted by. Michael had already left for a meeting. Amelia decided to wait to tell him about the video until she viewed it.

It's so peaceful here, she thought. *But conflicts and challenges are a part of being human, and they always will be. Now, with the internet, anything you say or do can spread like wildfire. How can I stop my strange ability from being sensationalized?*

Amelia went inside, turned on her computer, and opened Facebook. She was shocked to see a dozen friend requests. She checked out each one and realized she didn't know any of the people. One girl's request made her stop, and she clicked on the profile.

The solemn, lovely face of a young woman stared back at Amelia. Surprisingly, there was only a single photo, not dozens like on most profiles of people her age. Amelia stared into the dark eyes and accepted the friend request of Katrina Sanderson.

Next, she opened her email and clicked on the link Sasha had sent her. She watched the video of the community meeting, and the replay of her voicing the demand. The shocking part was seeing the look on Banner's face as he unintentionally told the truth.

"Holy crap," Amelia said aloud. "What the hell is going to happen now?" She forwarded the YouTube link to Michael, Lottie, and Ben, and then went back to Facebook. There was a private message from Katrina, who lived an hour south of the island on Jacksonville Beach. Amelia sent her a private message, and they made arrangements to meet the following day at a restaurant in the Navy seaside town of Mayport.

Amelia decided to head into Fernandina Beach and pick up a local newspaper. She wanted to make certain there was no mention of her in the paper. She parked on Centre Street, strolled down the tree-lined sidewalk, and dropped four quarters into the metal box at the corner. Her heart sunk when she saw there was a photo of Banner on the front page. Finding an empty park bench, she read through the article and was grateful there was no mention of the woman who had called out for Ronald to tell the truth.

The article stopped before Banner blurted out his true intentions. Amelia let out a sigh of relief, but she also felt a wave of anger.

"Why didn't they include what he really wants to do?" she said aloud.

A husky voice behind her answered, "Because there are local politicians who would allow it."

Amelia jumped and turned around to face an elderly bald man studying her with bright blue eyes behind large, plastic-rimmed glasses.

"Oh, my. I didn't mean to say that out loud."

"You were at the meeting, weren't you? You asked Banner to tell the truth."

Amelia blushed, folded the newspaper and got to her feet. "Yes. I hadn't meant to say that out loud, either."

"I'm Jasper Simpson. I didn't mean to startle you. I'm glad his intentions were made known. Too bad the reporter didn't tell the whole story. Banner looked like he'd been hit by a stun gun. He was choking on his words."

"It was unusual. I guess we'll have to see what happens next. I've got to go. Nice to meet you."

Jasper smiled and nodded. Amelia darted to her car and drove to the harbor. She was surprised to realize that the repairs from Hurricane Matthew were still not completed. There had been over $26,000,000 in damages to the island, even though the eye of the storm had been far off-shore. The hurricane in October had been followed by a national political tornado in November; nothing was quite what it had been before.

Amelia drove to North 14th Street and made her way to Bosque Bello Cemetery near Old Town Fernandina. She drove down winding, unpaved roads to the original section. She parked under an ancient oak and began to roam around the headstones. She'd always thought the graveyard looked like a perfect movie set, except this was real.

The quiet surroundings reminded her of the forest she and her friends had frequented when they were kids. The events of her NDE swirled in her mind, and she felt overwhelming gratitude that she'd returned from the other side.

CHAPTER 13

Katrina

I t was a beautiful drive along A1A from the island past the state parks of Big Talbot Island and Little Talbot Island. Amelia drove her car into the lineup for the ferry to take her across the St. John's River to Mayport. The quick ride was always a pleasure for her, and for her guests, whenever they visited. She got out of the car and stood by the railing, breathing in the fresh sea air. She was nervous about meeting a stranger she'd connected with on Facebook.

She entered the rustic seafood restaurant and looked around the room for Katrina. Amelia spotted the young woman at a window seat, peering out at the fishing boats moored in the river. She walked over and said hello.

Katrina jumped. "Oh, hi. I guess I'm a little nervous these days. Thanks for coming, Amelia. I think we have a lot in common."

Amelia sat across from the young woman with the wavy, chestnut-colored hair draped over her shoulders. There was a hint of sadness in her lovely, oval face.

"It's nice to meet you. You're the only friend request I accepted, and I'm not really sure why I did it," Amelia began. "I followed my intuition."

Katrina smiled. "I follow my intuition now more than ever. When I saw the YouTube video of you and the reaction of that builder, I wanted to meet you. I've recently acquired a few paranormal abilities of my own."

"Are you from Jax Beach?"

44

"Yeah, I was born and raised in the area. I can't imagine living anywhere else."

"My husband and I just recently moved here full time. We last lived in Boston. Our kids are scattered across the country."

"I haven't seen much of the US, but I'd like to take a road trip to California someday."

Amelia was curious about the young woman. "What abilities do you have now that you didn't have before?"

"Sometimes I can read people's minds. It's been really freaky. And I have premonitions. I'm not making it up."

"I believe you. I can't deny anymore that something unusual is going on with me, too. I just never expected it to be broadcast on social media. How did this happen to you?"

"Six months ago, I had an ADE—an actual-death experience. I was in a car crash. I was dead for three minutes before they got my heart going again." There was a far-away look in Katrina's eyes, and she was silent for a long moment.

"It was dark, then I opened my eyes and looked down at my body. I was surprisingly OK. I didn't care about the 'meat suit' below. I looked toward the sky, and a brilliant light drew me up. In an instant, I was flying over the most incredible scenery I had ever seen. Meadows of wildflowers gave way to verdant forests, thundering rivers, and magnificent water falls."

"Did you know where you were?" Amelia asked.

"It didn't take me long to figure out that I was in the spirit realm. I've been a student of world religions and spirituality for years. I graduated from college last year, and I've continued my studies on my own. I knew for sure where I was when I landed on the steps of a Greek temple and met two wise beings."

"Were they angels?"

"They were glowing with loving energy, but were more like wise teachers. They silently led me into the temple, and we entered a round chamber. Pictures of my life were playing on a three hundred sixty-degree panoramic screen. I began to notice that tiny stars would flash when something important was occurring."

"That's cool, Katrina. I've never heard of that happening."

"I hadn't either! It was like I was only there for a short time, and I needed to focus on the most important events. It was an intense learning experience. Then I was shown scenes from past lives that directly impacted my present lifetime."

"I've always wondered why humans can't access information from the past lives of their souls, and know about the true nature of our existence beyond what traditional religions teach," Amelia added.

"That's what I've been studying, Amelia. Religions have grains of truth. I feel caught between accepting the Catholic Church's dogma and a deeper search for spiritual truth."

"Two things that bother me," said Amelia, "are the notions that God should be feared, and that there's only one path to reach Him/Her. I don't think the Universal Power is female or male, and no belief system has a monopoly on the truth. Once again it's about mankind's endless desire for money, power, and control over others that fuels traditional religions."

"I get into so many arguments with people about this, yet I still believe there's a place for tradition."

"Is that why you wear a cross?"

Katrina lifted her hand to the gold cross that hung around her neck. "It was my grandmother's. I guess I wear it to remind me of her. And I've been grateful to Father Rathbone, at the Catholic Church in Jax Beach. He's the only other person I've told about my abilities since the accident. He visited me after I got home from the hospital."

"Wow, how did he respond?"

"He was unexpectedly open to what I told him. He said he believed that I believe, and that was enough."

"I'm glad he didn't make you feel you were crazy. Katrina, did you want to come back?"

"I was given the choice to return to my body or stay on the other side. I'm glad I decided to come back. I've been in touch with others like me on the internet. I can give you the sites, if you want. Actually, I had a premonition about meeting you. Amelia Island popped into my head over and over again. Now I know why."

"I had no idea I'd ever live on an island with my name. And thanks, I'd like to connect with others who've had NDEs or ADEs."

"It's been strange being able to read people's thoughts. I've wondered if the telepathy could go both ways: if I could plant ideas in others. At the moment, I can tell when people are lying, but I'm not able to make them tell the truth like you can."

Amelia was lost in thought. "What we're able to do is a huge responsibility. For me, it's totally foreign territory. Even seeing auras is something new."

"I see auras now, too. And do you find you're more sensitive to the energy of people around you? I can't stand being in crowds anymore. It feels like an assault on my personal space."

"I haven't been anywhere to really test that out yet. I was at the city hall meeting, but it wasn't a large crowd. Time will tell! Here's my card, if you ever need to get in touch," Amelia said, pressing the card into the young girl's hand.

"I can't tell you how much better I feel, just being able to talk to you in person."

* * *

While Katrina and Amelia were meeting, Father Rathbone slipped into the Opus Dei office in Jacksonville Beach. He retrieved a burner cell phone from a locked cabinet and sent a cryptic text to his partners. The three men had met at the Republican National Committee's winter meeting in January, at the Hotel Del Coronado in San Diego.

The text read: *Targets confirmed. Execution of KNC plan on course. Time to meet.*

CHAPTER 14

Spidey Sense

When Amelia arrived at home, Lyla was sitting on her front porch with a glass of wine in her hand. Amelia got out of her car and walked up to the house with a relieved smile.

"Hello, my friend," said Lyla, "would you care to join me?"

"Why, yes; that would be lovely. It's been an interesting day, and I'm glad you're here to talk about it." Amelia sat in the chair and accepted the glass of wine. "I'm surprised you didn't text me when I wasn't home."

"I had a feeling that you'd be here soon. I guess I have your sixth sense."

Amelia laughed. "Lottie calls it my 'spidey sense.' Today I met with a young woman who was clinically dead for a few minutes, and she came back with unusual gifts like I did. She said that are many of us these days who have returned with psychic abilities. She can read people's minds."

"That's strange—or maybe it isn't, given the present situation. Since we've gone from Stephen Colbert's truthiness to alternative facts, we may need a legion of people with powers to make everyone who has power and influence be honest. Very interesting!"

"You're right, Lyla. It seems that those who accept bold-faced lies only double down when they're presented with irrefutable facts. I guess that's part of human nature—that and reverting back to tribalism. But what can we do about it? Will they ever accept the truth?"

Lyla answered, "Probably not. If they're passing their horrific right-wing agenda they don't care about facts. It's a scary country right now."

The ladies sipped their wine. "Recognizing the danger of the situation is different from figuring out how to make things right," said Amelia. "What can we do to make the people on The Hill be honest? And look out for the best interests of all the citizens, not just themselves and the one percent?"

"I just don't know," said Lyla. "I think many people ignore the worst parts of the GOP because they're loyal to the party and the conservative message. On that count, I can't blame them. We're all products of our upbringing. Also, too many people buy into the repressive patriarchy that's the cornerstone of America. The feminist movement pushed against this, and now the patriarchs are pushing back."

"You're right. Since 9/11 there's been a move away from women's equality and what some see as the feminization of society. They believe we are weakened and that led to an attack on our soil. Yet, I get the feeling that with the more enlightened Republicans there's buyer's remorse. People who voted for the GOP and aren't racist or xenophobic may be the ones who help turn the tide in 2018," added Amelia.

Lyla asked, "What do you think about the women's movement? Will women finally be believed when they tell stories of sexual harassment and assault?"

"No one took T's accusers seriously before the election even after he was caught on tape admitting to assaulting women, so I'm not sure. Time will tell."

"Oh, I wanted to tell you, my niece is getting married in two weeks in Georgetown. Would you like to join me? Andy will be at a conference in Atlanta."

Amelia gasped, remembering her vision of being grabbed and thrown into a van in Washington. She shivered as the memory of an actual time that she was abducted went through her mind.

"I'm not sure. Can I let you know tomorrow?"

"Of course," answered Lyla. "I thought it would be a fun ladies weekend. My niece works for a senator from Virginia, and her fiancé is a lawyer for an NGO. They are in the thick of all this craziness."

"Is your daughter going?"

"Yes, and it would be great if you could meet her. Annabelle is flying in from Austin with her boyfriend. I wish she lived closer."

"I wish at least one of my kids lived here, but I doubt they ever will. Ben is the only real beach baby. Maybe if he gets a few more horrible, Boston winters with a hundred inches of snow he'll move south."

"I do not miss the snow—except at Christmas."

"Lyla, have you heard of a group called the KNC?"

"Not that I can recall."

Michael drove up and opened the garage with the remote. He grabbed a folding chair and joined the ladies on the front porch.

"Would you like some wine, Honey?" Amelia asked.

"No thanks. So, what have you two been up to?"

"I was asking your wife to go with me to my niece's wedding in DC in a couple of weeks," said Lyla. "And she hasn't said yes."

"You should go, Amelia. A change of scenery would be good for you."

Amelia hadn't told Michael about her vision. He worried enough about the actual things that had happened to her. She didn't want to cause him any more stress.

"Maybe you're right, love. OK, Lyla, I'm in. It'll be nice to meet Annabelle."

"Great! I'll let my niece know that I have a plus one. Andy will be happy too. He felt guilty about not being able to go. His boss has been erratic lately, and he wants to smooth the waters."

"I know all about that, Lyla," said Michael. "Yet, it's all worth it."

Amelia added, "I do love our new house."

"Me too," added Michael. "But I still like to travel. And I've booked a hotel in Savannah next weekend. It's been twenty years since we were there with the kids."

"Oh, great, Honey! You're right about me needing a change of scenery to take my mind off...everything."

"OK, where would you two like to go for dinner?" asked Michael.

"How about Ciaos?" said Lyla. "I'm in the mood for some great pasta."

"We've been to every restaurant on the Island. I'm glad there are so many great choices," said Michael.

CHAPTER 15

Savannah

On Friday afternoon, Michael and Amelia drove north on Highway 95 toward Savannah. Black clouds threatened a coming storm but the rain held off as they crossed the border into Georgia.

"You're quiet today," said Michael.

"There's been a lot on my mind. You'd think I'd be more relaxed after my NDE."

"What do you mean?"

"Well, I know for sure that death isn't the end, so that's not a worry. But I feel tense all the time. I can't watch violent movies or TV shows where there's death and destruction of people's lives. And documentaries of the horrors in our world send me over the edge."

"That's understandable," Michael added.

"But when I watch some of the new comedies that are mean spirited or just stupid, I feel like screaming."

"Maybe you should stay away from all media for a while."

Amelia laughed. "You're right. Even when I find a nice romantic comedy it seems mindless or ridiculous. I've never been like this before. I'm not sure if it's caused by the election or my accident."

"It's probably both."

"Thank goodness I can walk and meditate on the beach. It helps my low-grade anxiety. It really is like a low-grade fever. I don't feel terrible, but I also don't feel good."

"You should start riding your bike again in the Fort Clinch Park, or maybe down to Big Talbot Island. I'll have to replace the bike that disappeared from the moving van. I'm glad they gave us the full value of the bike in our claim."

"Me too. There's a mental health reason to find beauty in our daily life. Being in nature is important."

"We need a little humor too—and not just the political kind. Laughter is good medicine for the soul."

They drove in silence as wind-driven rain pounded the car. Amelia was mesmerized by the windshield wipers and went into a light trance. Once again, she had an unexpected vision.

Amelia was standing in a dimly lit room with a sliver of light coming through the windows. As her eyes adjusted to the soft light, she realized that she was in the Oval Office at the White House. She took a moment to look around and spotted a figure by one of the tall windows framed by pale blue drapes. It wasn't the current president. It was a woman with her back to Amelia.

Michael pushed on the car horn as a pickup truck cut him off. Amelia screamed and jumped in her seat. She took a deep breath and calmed her frazzled nerves.

"Sorry, were you sleeping?"

"No, not really. It was more like a trance. I was in the Oval Office, and I saw a woman standing by the window."

Michael paused before commenting. "Do you think it might be a premonition? Could the next president be a woman?"

"I hope so. I had the weirdest feeling that I was supposed to be there and I had an appointment. Why on earth would I have a vision about being asked to go to the White House?"

"You have an amazing imagination. You really need to write a book. It would be a chronicle of this unusual time."

The rain began to let up as they turned east on Highway 16. They entered the historic city of Savannah and drove past beautiful treed squares with fountains or statues gracing the centers. After several wrong turns, they finally found their hotel. They valet parked, checked in, and went to their chic, modern hotel room. After unpacking, they grabbed their umbrellas and headed out to explore the charming city.

They strolled through City Market and decided to take a trolley tour. The tour guide provided a traditional historical speech along with added personal anecdotes about growing up in the unique, eclectic city. They passed the Bonaventure Cemetery made famous by the novel and movie, *Midnight in the Garden of Good and Evil.* The guide indicated that the statue featured in the film had been moved to a museum for safekeeping.

"Fame is a double-edged sword," the guide began. "We need the tourism to keep the city vital, but too many people can damage the structure and corrupt the soul of a city. Sometimes we have to make tough choices about protecting our heritage."

The trolley passed nondescript government housing. "That housing is a blight on our city. It was the Federal Government's first attempt at bringing those people into society. Many of them were better off before the Civil War. At least they had a roof over their heads, food and something useful to do."

Michael whispered to Amelia, "Did he just say that blacks were better off as slaves? Did you make him say that?"

"No," answered Amelia. "He's a racist all on his own. I can't believe he'd say that to a group of tourists."

"He's not getting a tip from me after the tour."

Amelia glared at the guide as she exited the trolley. He scowled back at her, and she knew that nothing she said would change his prejudiced heart. Amelia and Michael walked to Leopold's Ice Cream store and joined the lineup outside.

"The old-fashioned soda fountain in here is great. Do you want ice cream or a float?" Michael asked.

"I'm going to blow the diet and get a sundae. That tour guide's comments were just awful. It reminded me of my tour of Andrew Jackson's home in Nashville several years ago. The guide talked glowingly about the paintings of their generals and the fact that the South may someday rise again."

"It's shocking, Honey. Still not sure how we can change the minds of people who simply hate anyone who's different."

CHAPTER 16

Bridges

D inner at the Rose House Inn was spectacular. The Victorian home was filled with lovely antiques, but the menu was decidedly nouvelle cuisine. Traditional Lowcountry specialties were given a modern twist, and Amelia and Michael savored every morsel. After dinner they strolled along River Street, peering into the shops that had been converted from old cotton warehouses.

"Michael, look at that beautiful amethyst! The large one on the wood base."

Without answering, Michael entered the store, picked up the large stone and took it to the cashier. He returned to Amelia, standing outside with her jaw hanging open.

"Oh my gosh! Thanks, Honey. I have the perfect spot for it, on the bookshelf in the great room." She took the plastic bag and placed it in the large tote she always used for travelling. "This is really heavy."

They sauntered further down the cobblestone street and ended up in a darkened area where the streetlights were broken. They were about to turn around and move toward the busier section when a group of young men wearing baseball caps and Confederate T-shirts passed them. Michael turned his head to see where they were going and noticed a slender man walking toward the group.

The man tried to quickly walk past the youths, but one of the young men grabbed the older gentleman, punched him in stomach, and threw him to the ground.

"Get out of my country, Muslim!" the youth screamed. Some of the others started kicking the man lying on the pavement, as he shielded himself from the blows. Michael rushed over and grabbed two of the boys and shoved them away.

"Stop it! What the hell are you doing?" Michael yelled.

The young tattooed thug who first attacked the man turned around and punched Michael in the face. Amelia rushed over, and with a mighty swing she hit Michael's attacker in the face with her tote bag. The large amethyst rock smashed into his head, sending the youth tumbling to the ground. Michael recovered enough to grab two of the other boys and knock them together. He grabbed another one by the collar and raised his fist to punch him. The boy screamed and tried to cover his face.

Michael flung the boy to the ground. The gang of racist brutes staggered away, leaving a trail of profanities in their wake. Amelia helped the gentleman to his feet.

"Thank you both so much. This is the third time since the election that I've been attacked. And I'm not a Muslim! Having brown skin makes me a target in this neo-fascist society."

"We're sorry you have to go through this," said Amelia. "It just keeps getting worse. The Republicans have released a white supremacist monster. When will it end?"

"I am Eshan Baht. Violence is never the answer. We must continue to go the way of the peaceful warrior."

"I'm Michael Jones, and this is my wife, Amelia. I'm glad we were here at the right time. Though my jaw's going to be sore tomorrow."

"Thank you again, Mr. and Mrs. Jones. You are both very brave." Mr. Baht smiled and hurried away.

"Well that was more excitement than I needed tonight. Let's head back to the hotel," said Michael.

"I'm really glad you bought me the amethyst. It made a great weapon. Although, it's ironic that a stone known for its peaceful spiritual vibration was used in an act of violence."

The following morning, Michael and Amelia wandered through the city and ended up on River Street once again. They decided to have brunch at a table beside the window in a cozy restaurant and watched the tourists go by as they ordered. Amelia gazed at the massive suspension bridge that crossed the Savannah River.

"I can't stop thinking about how important it is to learn from the past, and bring that knowledge and wisdom into the present," Amelia began. "When we have the right foundation to build on, we can reimagine the future."

"I get you. It's like Picasso; he learned how to paint in a traditional style before he was able to create a completely new way of painting. He had the fundamentals down first."

"That's very perceptive, Michael. Like the bridge over there, people had to create simple structures before they could imagine and build a bridge like that one."

The server brought their meals then, and they were both lost in thought as they ate their Belgian waffles covered in berries and whipped cream.

"People can be bridges too, like Martin Luther King, Jr. and Nelson Mandela. They formed a link between the past, present, and a different future. Maybe that's what you can write about," Michael said.

"I'm not sure I get it," Amelia answered.

"You can research different bridges from a variety of time periods, then talk about someone from that era who was a game changer. MLK and the Edmund Pettus Bridge; Gandhi crossing a bridge over the Ganges River."

"I see what you're saying. Covered bridges and others; internal and external bridges; sound structures and crumbling infrastructures."

A noisy group of people entered the restaurant, followed by a local news crew. A grey-haired man shook hands with patrons and greeted several he obviously knew. A server approached Amelia's table.

"That's the congressman. He was the only one in Georgia who held a town hall meeting last February."

The news cameraman and several people using their phones captured the exchange between the congressman and his constituents. A woman called to him from her table, "Congressman, why do you still support that tyrannical Russian puppet?"

"Those of you who have studied the Bible know that God has used imperfect people to do great things before," the congressman answered.

The woman wasn't mollified. "But does God support a treasonous man who colluded with an enemy to get elected?"

"Good question," Michael said. The cameraman turned his camera on the Joneses. "What's your answer to that, sir?" Michael asked.

Amelia felt the vibration coursing through her body. "The truth be told," she said loud and clear. "Congressman, the truth be told."

The congressman visibly shuddered. He coughed several times. His eyes were laser focused on Amelia.

"Who cares what God thinks? The Russians helped the GOP get into power, and now we can do whatever the hell we want. And money follows power," the congressman growled.

Everyone in the room gasped. The politician looked around in shock. He rushed out of the restaurant, the news crew swiftly following. The embarrassed look on the legislator's face was priceless.

"You did it again, Amelia!" Michael whispered.

CHAPTER 17

The List

Father Rathbone pulled into the arrivals area at Jacksonville airport. He spotted Dr. Edgar Gabriel and swerved toward the curb. The good Doctor of Divinity from Freedom University in Virginia threw his suitcase in the back seat and got in the passenger side. The men drove to a secure location where the third member of the Knights of the New Crusade was waiting.

Dr. Gabriel swept the room for listening devices, still not confident of his new partners.

"You don't trust us?" Father Rathbone said gruffly.

"I can't take the chance of blindly believing in anyone these days."

"Come on, Doc," added Reverend Josh Miller. "I know I can trust y'all, and you can trust me. Let's get this meetin' goin'. I got a plane to catch back to St. Louis," he drawled.

"I didn't realize people from St. Louis had such, ah, strong accents," Father Rathbone said. "I thought that the first time we met."

Miller laughed. "That's 'cause I'm a Mississippi man who moved up the mighty river. The Lutheran seminary is in St. Louis, and I've been livin' there since I graduated."

They opened their computers and went to a shared file. There were six names listed, with complete biographies on each person. A second document listed the strength and weaknesses of four men and two women. These were leading Democrats expected to run for president in 2020.

"Can we narrow this list down? If we get it down to three, we can each take care of one of them," said Dr. Gabriel.

"Who would've thought an Evangelical, a Catholic and a Lutheran would be workin' together," marveled Miller. "Bizarre times."

"Desperate times require desperate measures. The progress we've made cannot and will not be destroyed. Even if the left gains some power in 2018, we won't let the godless heathens erase what we've achieved," said Dr. Gabriel.

"Once the targets are identified, we should only refer to them by code names," Rathbone declared.

The men had initially met at the Rising Stars Townhall Meeting at the RNC's winter conference in Southern California. Examining the best talent on the right spurred the idea that the left had their stars for 2020. Over dinner and several drinks, a plot was hatched that would eliminate the greatest threat from the other political party and intimidate those remaining.

CHAPTER 18

Connor

A melia and Michael arrived home the following morning. Amelia went into the kitchen and opened her laptop. She typed in the congressman's name on Google, and saw a newsfeed of what happened in Savannah the day before.

The anchor of the local station mentioned Amelia's name. The YouTube video of the city hall meeting with the developer was also on the first page of results. Michael came up behind her as she played both clips again. The doorbell rang soon after, and they looked at one another. Amelia stormed down the hall and swung open the door, expecting a reporter. Katrina was nervously peering around.

"Katrina, come in," said Amelia.

"I'm sorry. I should have called. I...I didn't know who else to talk to." The distress in her voice was palpable. Amelia led her to the great room.

"Please have a seat. Would you like some tea? Michael, this is Katrina. I met her in Mayport last week."

"Of course," said Michael. "Nice to meet you. I'll be in the office if you need me." Michael grabbed an energy drink and left the room. Amelia filled the kettle with water, then took out mugs, plates, and a box of shortbread cookies. She placed tea bags in a china teapot, and carried everything to the coffee table on a silver tray. Making tea was a soothing ritual for her.

"I guess you saw the news. The local Savannah newscast of you and the congressman went national," Katrina started. "How are you doing?"

"Actually, we just got home and saw it. What happens next is anyone's guess. It's astonishing how quickly something spreads on social media, and in the regular media."

"I guess to my generation it isn't surprising at all. We've grown up wired. We panic when we're *not* connected."

Amelia poured the tea and offered a mug to her visitor. She set out the cookies and settled into the large sectional sofa. Both women were quiet for several minutes.

"My psychic abilities keep getting stronger. I can not only read people's minds, I get flashes of deep, dark secrets, too" said Katrina.

Amelia was startled. "Do you sense anything about me?"

"Yeah, you were harmed in the past by a horrible man. But you saved yourself. It could have been even worse. Is that correct?"

"Yes. It's something I don't like to think about. But you're on the right track. Is that why you're here? To ask me about my past?"

"No, and I didn't mean to upset you. I wanted to show you what's been happening to me. Several people have approached me wanting help to find loved ones, or asking me to read minds and see if a person was truthful."

"Are you worried about something specific?"

Katrina took a deep breath and played with the gold cross at her neck. "Maybe this is what the future will look like. When people can read each other's minds and there are no secrets, we'll have a peaceful society. We'll all instantly know when we're in danger."

"Katrina, are you in danger?"

The young woman stood and began pacing in front of the fireplace. "I might be. This guy, Connor Stewart, a friend of a friend, contacted me about locating his missing motorcycle. I met with him and the coworker he suspected of stealing the bike."

"Was the coworker guilty?" asked Amelia.

"No, and I told him that. But when I was talking to Connor afterward, I got a clear impression of a serious crime he'd committed years before. He'd raped and murdered a girl, then dumped her body in a river. It might be the St. Mary's River."

"Dear God! What did you say?"

"I didn't tell him I knew! I guess I had a shocked look on my face before I bolted. He must have known something was up, because he keeps calling and texting me. I'm scared he'll silence me before I can figure out what to do."

"Do you have the girl's name or any other details?"

"It was Annie or Abby, something like that, and about six or seven years ago."

"You've got to go to the police. Do you have relatives out of state that you can stay with?"

Katrina flopped on the sofa. "No, not really. My mom's an only child like me. My dad's been out of the picture for years. My grandparents passed away a long time ago."

"Does Connor know where you live?"

"Yeah, and I think he's stalking me."

Amelia got up and went into the office to talk to Michael. After a short conversation with her husband, she returned to the family room. "OK, I have an idea. Michael's cousin, Marilyn, runs a women's shelter in Philadelphia. You can give a full account to the police, then head directly to Philly. Our son Sasha is there too, if you need anything."

"I don't want to put your family in danger!"

"Don't worry, Marilyn's used to this type of situation. She's trustworthy and capable. She'll help you for as long as you need," Amelia answered. "Tell your employer you need vacation time. Don't tell anyone where you're going. Do you have enough money for the trip?"

Tears pooled in Katrina's eyes. Amelia walked to the pantry and brought out a box of tissues. She sat beside the young woman and briefly hugged her.

"Yeah, I have a savings account. I didn't know this new ability would bring danger! I can't believe this is happening. I'm really scared."

"Should I call Marilyn?"

"I guess so. What else can I do? I'll stay away until the cops figure out who the victim is, and they can haul Connor's ass in."

CHAPTER 19

Blue Lies

Amelia was relieved that the only contacts she'd received about the YouTube video, and newscast about the congressman, were through Facebook. She wasn't sure how long it would be until reporters were knocking on her door.

She was thankful when Katrina sent a text saying she was on her way to Philadelphia, after meeting with the Jacksonville police. She also said that she'd texted Father Rathbone to let him know she'd miss a follow-up meeting with him. *One problem solved; how many more are to come?* Amelia wondered.

The next text she received was from Ruby, inviting her and Michael to see a stand-up comedian performing at a local theater. Amelia responded that she'd check their schedule, but it sounded like a great idea. Ruby said that she'd seen the comedian before and thought he was funny, even if his language was a little blue.

Blue...Blue language, blue lies. Where did I hear something about blue lies? Amelia went online and Googled the phrase. *Oh my gosh! Linda said something about this right before I came back. Now I remember...and here's an article on the* Scientific American *website.*

'How the Science of "Blue Lies" May Explain T's Support

They're a very particular form of deception that can build solidarity within groups.

By Jeremy Adam Smith

T tells lies.

His deceptions and misleading statements are easy to unmask. In the latest example—after hundreds of well-documented lies—FBI director James Comey told Congress this week that there is "no information that supports" T's claim that President Obama tapped his phone.

But T's political path presents a paradox. Far from slowing his momentum, his deceit seemed only to strengthen his support through the primary and national election. Now, every time a lie is exposed, his support among Republicans doesn't seem to waver very much. In the wake of the Comey revelations, his average approval rating held at 40 percent.

This has led many people to ask themselves: How does the former reality-TV star get away with it? How can he tell so many lies and still win support from many Americans?

Journalists and researchers have suggested many answers, from hyperbiased, segmented media to simple ignorance on the part of GOP voters. But there is another explanation that no one seems to have entertained. It is that T is telling 'blue lies'—a psychologist's term for falsehoods, told on behalf of a group, that can actually strengthen the bonds among the members of that group.

Children start to tell selfish lies at about age three, as they discover adults cannot read their minds: *I didn't steal that toy, Daddy said I could, He hit me first.* At around age seven, they begin to tell white lies motivated by feelings of empathy and compassion: *That's a good drawing, I love socks for Christmas, You're funny.*

Blue lies are a different category altogether, simultaneously selfish and beneficial to others—but only to those who belong to your group. As University of Toronto psychologist Kang Lee explains, blue lies fall in between generous white lies and selfish 'black' ones. "'You can tell a blue lie against another group,'" he says, which makes it simultaneously selfless and self-serving. "'For example, you can lie about your team's cheating in a game, which is antisocial, but helps your team.'"

In a 2008 study of seven, nine, and 11-year-old children—the first of its kind—Lee and colleagues found that children become more likely to endorse and tell blue lies as they grow older. For example, given an opportunity to lie to an interviewer about rule-breaking in the selection process of a school chess team, many were quite willing to do so, older kids more than younger ones. The children telling this lie didn't stand to selfishly benefit; they were doing it on behalf of their school. This line of research finds that black lies drive people apart, white lies draw them together, and blue lies pull some people together while driving others away."

Amelia's cell phone rang in her pocket, making her jump. She'd had several calls from unknown numbers, and she thought it was another stranger wanting to talk to her about her sudden fame on social media. She was pleased to see the caller was her wonderful son, Ben.

"Hey, Momma, how's it going?"

"Ben! Perfect timing. I had another memory from my NDE. Linda said something about blue lies, and I'd never heard the term. There was an online article about it that really makes sense."

"I've never heard of blue lies. What are they?"

"Well, you've heard of little white lies told so you don't hurt someone's feelings. And black lies are outright untruths told for selfish reasons. Here, I'll read the description: 'It is that T is telling "blue lies"—a psychologist's term for falsehoods, told on behalf of a group, that can actually strengthen the bonds among the members of that group.' That's why so many Republicans believe his endless bullshit."

"But don't they see through it?" Ben asked.

"Apparently not. Simon and Garfunkel wrote, 'A man hears what he wants to hear and disregards the rest.' It seems to be part of human nature to defend whatever your social group tells you."

"Yeah, you're right. S and G also wrote, 'And the people bowed and prayed to the neon god they'd made.' Prophetic guys."

"This election has brought out the very best and very worst of humanity. What a time we live in," Amelia added. "It's also a study in psychology. Deplorables, dupes and believers in blue lies."

"And these people still support a dictator wannabe, whose daughter and son-in-law want to help run the White House. Sick nepotism," added Ben.

"Maybe that's why Ruby invited your dad and me to see a stand-up comic. We need to lighten our spirits."

"I was thinking about humor yesterday, and how comedians have dealt with all this. There are two late night shows on the same network with totally different takes. One makes lame jokes about trivial things. The other has biting satire that lets you know it's OK to be outraged. And he's the one the alt-right wants fired."

"Honey, there are audiences for both types of shows. Sometimes the enormity of the situation can swamp the senses and light humor is welcome. But ignoring or normalizing this administration is not an option."

CHAPTER 20

Premonitions

A dark shadow crossed Amelia's heart when she read that the Syrian dictator had murdered his own citizens with poison nerve gas. Just days before the attack, the US Secretary of State had signaled his support of the Syrian tyrant, and said the Syrian people had to decide whether he should stay or go.

The lunatic in the White House blamed the previous president, saying, as usual, that he inherited a mess. It was lost on the orange emperor that he'd constantly railed against intervention in Syria in the past. Hypocrisy was on display every single day. He'd flip-flopped so many times on everything from NATO to China that it made heads spin and stomachs churn.

I knew people would die after this election. More than 200 civilians were killed in Iraq by American air strikes. There were almost 100 innocent Syrians blown apart as they were trying to flee the country in buses. Where's the GOP outrage like after Benghazi, where four people died? Did the Russians instigate this atrocious action in Syria to draw the US into war? Or is it a Wag the Dog situation, where 45 is trying to distract from the treasonous actions of his gang of traitors? What happens if they try and move the US Embassy from Tel Aviv to Jerusalem, like they talked about on the campaign trail? What will the Palestinians do?

And why did we bomb an almost empty airstrip and use the most powerful non-nuclear bomb in Afghanistan? The war-mongering Republicans call the bombings great actions, and the mainstream media sucks it up! Now 45's inviting the worst murderous dictators in the world to the White House; he says he'd be 'honored' to meet with that insane North Korean butcher!

Amelia opened her Facebook account to see she had sixty-seven friend requests. She was about to delete her account when she heard the words *not yet* in her mind. She turned off the computer and decided she needed to walk along the shore to calm her nerves. The amount of free-floating stress hormones in her system was alarming.

She drove to the north end of the island, where 80-year-old beach shacks dotted the shoreline. Newer homes were interspersed throughout the area, known for its laidback lifestyle. Surfers in pickup trucks passed her and parked on the level sand beside the dunes.

Pulling into a parking lot, she hopped out and strolled over the wooden boardwalk to the ocean. To the north was a fishing pier in the state park that had been damaged by the hurricane, and was now being demolished. They were dredging the mouth of the river to ensure it was deep enough for the nuclear subs to get to King's Bay, Georgia. Amelia headed in that direction, combing the sand for sharks' teeth. She thought she'd found one, but on closer inspection realized it was an arrowhead.

Amelia joyfully pocketed the treasure from the sea, wondering how old this relic of the Timucuan Native Americans was. She waded into the water as the gentle waves lapped against her legs. Closing her eyes, she slipped into a light trance. She had a vision of a bucolic scene with people riding bicycles down country roads. Lush, rolling hills rose above a peaceful village. Children were playing in gardens while elderly women kept watch.

Suddenly, there was a loud whistling noise and everyone looked skyward. A massive rocket zoomed toward the village. There was a deafening explosion. Bodies and debris flew into the air. Amelia screamed and was jolted out of her vision. She gasped for air and stumbled out of the water. Doubled-over, she caught her breath then headed for the car. She grabbed a notebook and wrote down everything she could remember from the vision.

Later that evening, she poured two glasses of Chianti and turned on her computer to FaceTime with the Sassy Seekers. Lyla arrived just as they were beginning the conversation. Amelia set the computer on the kitchen island so they could both see the ladies in Boston—Angela, Emily, and Barbara—who had gathered at Angie's house.

Angela's jovial, round face, framed by curly brown hair, filled the screen. "Hello there, Amelia. You're looking great, considering. And thanks for the email describing your NDE. What an amazing story!"

"Thanks, Angie."

"We were all so worried about you. And welcome, Lyla! We're looking forward to hearing all about you."

"It's great to be here. I'm excited about learning from you lovely ladies," said Lyla. "I haven't studied very much about religion or spirituality, but I've been doing a lot of praying lately."

"Me too," Barb added. "I'm not sure it will do any good, but it's worth a try. The world feels like it's on the brink of disaster."

Angela's expression became grim, and she began the conversation with the question, "Is anyone else having disturbing nightmares? I feel like my soul's being assaulted on a nightly basis."

"I do, for sure," said Emily. Her platinum blond hair lit up the screen. "Everything is out of whack, in my dreams and the real world. Where's the 'New Earth' that was coming in 2012? What happened to the age of enlightenment, with humanity moving toward peace, kindness, and compassion?"

No one answered for a long time. "We're spiritual seekers who've had to face a physical world of growing militarism and attacks on basic civility and truth. Not to mention the dumbing down of the country, and the increasing power of the wealthy to screw the masses and trash the environment. No wonder we're all having nightmares," said Angela.

"I have an ongoing battle with myself," added Barbara, "whether to watch all the horrible news or tune out completely. I'm trying to find a balance for my own sanity, but I can't ignore what's happening." Barbara was petite, with Asian features and dark, piercing eyes.

The women in both Massachusetts and Florida reached for a glass of wine at the same moment. A round of laughter followed when they realized their common need for a little vino.

"Earlier today, when I was at the beach, I had a vision. It was like a mini nightmare," Amelia began. She proceeded to tell them of the frightening images of a village being bombed.

"Oh my gosh, Amelia! I had a dream the other night of a similar landscape. I was wearing a kimono and pouring tea. A sense of dread overcame me, and I went outside to check on my children. A moment later there was this horrible sound and a bomb obliterated everything! I woke up in a sweat," said Barbara.

"Barb, do you think you were in Japan?" Amelia asked.

"Yes, I'm sure of it. Are these premonitions? Did I have this dream because my grandmother is Japanese?"

Amelia answered, "I really don't know."

"And if they are premonitions," Emily began, "does it mean that they're inevitable? Or is it one possible future that can be changed, like Scrooge's vision of what was to come was altered?"

"It's interesting that Linda mentioned Scrooge during my NDE. There are so many possibilities and unanswered questions."

Lyla leaned into the computer's camera. "Do any of you attend regular church services?"

They all shook their heads no. "I miss the rituals and community of the church, but I couldn't agree with their stance on reproduction rights," said Emily.

"Outside of weddings and funerals, I haven't been to services in decades," Amelia added. "I tried several progressive churches, but nothing quite fit."

"Are we a spiritually lost group, or a more discerning one?" asked Barbara. "Those who blindly follow religion and their political parties are not doing the world any favors."

"How can we ensure a separation of church and state like the founding fathers insisted upon?" added Lyla. "Especially since they're trying to give people the right to discriminate against the LGBTQ community on religious grounds?"

"And yet," Amelia began, "there are millions of people defying the system and stepping up to protest the most despicable aspects of the administration. There is hope."

Lyla added, "But will enough enlightened Democrats run for office and get out the vote in the midterms? In 2016, only half of eligible voters actually voted. How do we connect with even a medium-size percentage of the millions who didn't vote?"

"And the Republicans who can no longer defend the president, and may join the resistance," added Emily. "How do we engage them?"

CHAPTER 21

The Accident

Strolling down Centre Street, Amelia received a text from Marilyn saying that Katrina had arrived safely in Philly and was doing well. She then got a text from Ruby stating that the comedian they were supposed to see had cancelled his appearance due to illness. *Maybe the comic just can't be funny right now.* There was a tap on her shoulder and she spun around to face a young woman.

"You're Mrs. Jones, aren't you? I'm a reporter for the local news website *The Fernandina Insider*. I saw you at the city hall meeting and on YouTube."

Amelia smiled and strode away.

"I'm Teresa Salinger," she said as she walked beside the older woman. "I'd like to talk to you off the record. It's a really important personal matter. Can I buy you a cup of coffee?"

She looked into Teresa's troubled eyes and made a quick decision. "OK, the coffee shop is on the next block."

The women silently walked into the crowded store. There was an empty high-top table in the back, and Teresa dropped her backpack on one of the chairs. She returned and stood in line beside Amelia. They brought their drinks to the table and Teresa fidgeted with her latte.

"I don't normally talk to strangers, Teresa but you seem anxious. I followed my intuition and decided to hear you out. So, how can I help you?"

"It's not about me. It's about my aunt and cousin. And from what I saw with my own eyes and the follow up stories about you online, I *know* you can make people tell the truth."

"What's going on?"

Teresa swirled sugar into her latte. Her long, strawberry-blond hair fell over her face. She took a deep breath, flipped her hair behind her ears and looked up at Amelia.

"My Uncle Jason died three years ago. My Aunt Marcia became involved with a man named Marvin six months ago. My cousin Jessie was worried this creep was just trying to get money from her mom. She had him checked out by a private investigator. The PI didn't find anything, but we don't trust Marvin. He can be charming, but I just know he's a psychopath."

"How can I help?"

"He talked Aunt Marcia into eloping last month!" Teresa's voice became loud and agitated. "Then, last week, they were driving back from St. Augustine, and he crashed his car into a tree. He's OK, but my aunt's in a coma."

Tears pooled in the young woman's eyes. Amelia took her hand. "You probably know that I was in a coma and I'm fine now."

"Yeah, I heard about you when I was visiting my aunt at the hospital. Jessie and I believe that it wasn't an accident, that Marvin purposely ran into the tree to kill her. She'd added him to her will against her lawyer's wishes. But there's no way we can prove it."

"I'm so sorry, but I still don't see how I can help."

"If you come to the hospital when he's there, you can make him tell the truth! You can ask him what happened the night of the accident, and he'll have to answer honestly. I can be there and record it. Then we can take his confession to the cops."

"Oh, jeez, I don't know. I'm not sure it would work, or if I should get involved."

"Please help us! We're worried that he's going to finish the job and kill my aunt somehow. Then he could go after Jessie. Aunt Marcia inherited a lot of money. This really is life and death!"

"Can I think about it, Teresa?"

"Yes, yes of course. I'll make sure there are other people in the room to back up what happens. Here's my card. Please call me when you decide."

Two days later, Amelia joined Teresa and Jessie at the hospital. It was disconcerting for Amelia to be back where she'd had her near-death experience. She bumped into Drew, the orderly who was in her room the night the doctor and nurse spoke of her ability and called her a witch.

Amelia told Marvin she was an old high school friend of Marcia's. Jessie had sent an email with details about Marcia's teen years, and Amelia regaled them with light-hearted stories. Marvin was a handsome, stout man with greying temples and deep-set eyes. He was overly charming and sickly sweet to Amelia. He obviously didn't recognize her from social media.

Jessie corroborated the tales of her mother in high school, and Teresa soon signaled Amelia that it was time to ask about the accident. With the recorder running, Amelia said, "I'm sorry that your lovely wife is in this awful state. But Marcia's such a strong, determined woman. I know she'll pull through."

"God willing," said Marvin as he faked concern. "If only I hadn't fallen asleep at the wheel! How can I ever forgive myself, if my darling Marcia never wakes up?"

Amelia smiled sadly and placed her hand on his tanned arm. His clammy skin revolted her, but she stuck to the script. "What actually happened the night of the accident? Marvin, the truth be told."

Marvin shivered, then pulled away from Amelia's touch. He began to shake and fearfully looked around the room at the expectant faces.

"I had to do it!" he muttered. "I knew Marcia was getting suspicious. I had to stop her from snooping into my past with other wealthy women. I took the chance of hurting myself by running into that tree. But she had to be stopped—permanently." Marvin gasped. Teresa bolted from the room with the recorder in hand.

Drew had been right outside the room, recording the events on his phone. Teresa almost knocked him down as she ran out the door.

CHAPTER 22

Center Stage

After telling Michael about her experience at the hospital, Amelia was exhausted. He poured her a glass of wine and suggested she relax in a nice, hot bath. When she was settled in the sudsy water, Amelia began to calm her jangled nerves. Candlelight danced around her as she once again drifted into a light trance.

She was standing in a darkened theater. A spotlight illuminated the stage. A figure in a dark cape with a fedora pulled low over his face entered. He walked to center stage, raised his head, and glared at her. "It's a holy war!" the man called out. He took off the hat and pulled out a small, white rabbit. He placed the bunny on the stage, laughed eerily, and watched it hop away. He disappeared in a puff of smoke.

Amelia gasped and came out of her trance. She quickly got out of the tub and wrapped a large towel around herself as she tried to make sense of the images. Michael entered the bathroom hearing his wife talking to herself.

"Honey, what's wrong?"

She dropped into the vanity chair and took a deep breath. "I just had the strangest vision, or dream or whatever. I was in a dark theater and a sinister man came onto the stage. He said there's a holy war. He took a rabbit out of his hat, then he disappeared. Oh my gosh, it was the vice president!"

"You have one vivid imagination. What could it mean?"

"I have no idea what any of my visions mean. It's time for bed."

Amelia slid under the covers and reflected on her visions. She shivered, even though the comforter was tucked up to her chin. It was like something took over her mind when she had a vision, and it wasn't a comfortable feeling. She was concerned that she felt a loss of control over her own body, and worried it would occur more frequently and at inopportune times.

The following morning, news vans were parked outside the house when Michael left for a meeting. Reporters called out to him as he hopped into his car and drove away. Amelia was still in her robe when the doorbell rang at the same time as her cell phone. She answered the phone and her husband warned her about the press outside. She ignored the doorbell and went into her bedroom, closed the blinds, and turned on the local news.

There it was. A reporter at the Fernandina police station on Lime Street described the arrest of one Marvin Darby after his step-niece brought in a recording of his confession to the attempted murder of his wife. The reporter had also interviewed orderly Drew Cavendish, who identified Amelia Jones as the person who prompted the confession. There was also mention of other occasions when Mrs. Jones made people speak the truth, seemingly against their best interests.

The house phone rang and startled Amelia. She unplugged the phone and opened her computer. She had over 100 friend requests on Facebook, and decided to delete her account. No one whispered in her ear this time to keep it open. Her cell phone received multiple calls; each one was an unknown number. She needed to vent, so she called Lottie.

"Hey, Mum, what's up?"

"Hi, Sweetie. Unfortunately, my fifteen minutes of fame has arrived. There are news vans outside the house, and my name was on the local report this morning."

"How did this happen?" Lottie asked.

"Yesterday I helped a young woman get a confession from her step-uncle that he tried to kill her aunt. Teresa recorded what he said and took it to the police. It was enough to get him arrested. An orderly at the hospital revealed my identity and the other times I was able to make someone tell the truth. What's next?"

"Good God, Mum! What are you going to do?"

"I'm not sure. I deleted my Facebook account, unplugged the house phone, and I'm going to change my cell number. I'm glad I put my car in the garage last night. I'm meeting Lyla at the library this morning; hopefully I can avoid the reporters."

"Be careful. There are so many nuts out there. And I don't mean the press. People fear what they don't understand. Call me later. Love you."

Amelia was about to leave when she got a call from Sasha. She filled him in on the unusual recent events.

"Are you scared, Mom?" Sasha asked.

"I have to admit I am. So many things are out of my control. I'm meeting Lyla in a while, and just going into town is a challenge."

"I won't keep you, but I wanted to tell you about a book on psychopaths I just finished. It's *The Bully's Trap*, by Andrew Faas. If you have a minute, I'll read you the main headings."

"Sure, Sasha. I have time."

"Tell me if you think they apply to 45. One, they have sadistic motives and intents. Two, they have a grandiose estimation of self. Three, they're glib, and constantly turn on superficial charm. Four, they're confident—even in the face of overwhelming evidence. Five, they're pathological liars. Six, they don't think the rules apply to them, and flaunt social norms and rules. Seven, they live a parasitic life. Eight, they are cunning and manipulative, masters of manipulation, deflection, and deception. Nine, they had early behavioral problems. Ten, they don't feel emotions like normal people. Eleven, their long-term goals are not realistic. Twelve, they show no remorse or guilt. Thirteen, they have a scary temper. Fourteen, they have a proclivity for non-committal relationships. Fifteen, they're often bored.'"

"Oh, my gosh. He's a classic narcissist! It's amazing—and terrifying."

"I'll let you go. Just wanted to share that with you."

"Thanks, Sweetie. I'll talk to you soon."

Amelia got ready to leave and jumped into her car. Opening the garage door, she carefully backed out amid reporters yelling questions at her. She drove away without hitting anyone. At the phone store, she had her cell number changed.

Lyla was pulling into the parking lot when Amelia arrived. Without a word, they walked past the library and headed to the coffee shop. They ordered their drinks and took them to the high-top table in the back of the restaurant where Amelia had met with the reporter.

"So, I thought the important news today was the continuing saga of the fired FBI director. In my book, your story overshadows the Russian investigation," said Lyla.

Amelia laughed and shook her head. "Only in this little corner of Florida. I'm grateful there's important national news. Are there tapes, or aren't there tapes? Then there's finally the admission that there are no tapes. Could the obstruction of justice charge finally bring down the orange clown?"

"We can only hope," Lyla answered. "So tell me what happened at the hospital."

The details of the previous evening's events were told between sips of coffee and bites of blueberry scones. "There's no doubt that you'll continue to be hounded by the press and others wanting your help. Are you ready?"

"Just like Katrina, this ability has thrown me for a loop. She's in real danger, and I hope it doesn't happen to me. Being the center of attention in the media only fans the flames and brings out the crazies. No one is ever ready for that."

"Are you still up to going to the wedding in DC with me?"

"Of course. I wouldn't let you down."

CHAPTER 23

Gardenia

Amelia thought about Lyla's question as she drove home. On one hand, she looked forward to escaping the local press until another breaking story drew them away. But the memories of her visions about being in the Oval Office, being thrown into a van in front of the White House, and the creepy image of the VP, troubled her.

She knew the trip to DC was important to Lyla, and getting away from the media was advisable. Driving past the news vans camped in front of her house solidified her decision. Once inside the safety of her home, she emailed her old friend Indira Batas, who lived in Reston, Virginia and worked in the capital. *Maybe a spiritual teacher can help me with the unusual psychic ability I now possess.*

She divulged the content of her visions and gave a full account of her new talent. Indira was intrigued, and told Amelia that she'd meditate on her friend's predicament. She hoped to have some insight and advice by the time Amelia arrived the following week.

Amelia booked her flight to arrive a day before Lyla would be flying to Ronald Reagan National Airport. She forwarded her schedule to Michael and her children, wanting them to know where she'd be and when. She then went on the internet and read an article on the local news site about Marvin Darby. It stated that Marcia remained in stable condition, but was still in a coma. Teresa wrote about the details of her aunt's relationship with Darby, and that she had found information about the despicable man that the private investigator couldn't or wouldn't provide.

There was also a paragraph about local resident Amelia Jones, and her ability to make people speak the truth. It was suggested that her recent accident and coma might have triggered this capability. There was a quote by an island psychic, Felicity Henderson, who corroborated that paranormal gifts were possible after people crossed the barrier between this world and the spirit world during a coma.

Amelia went on Felicity's website and sent her a message asking to meet the following morning. They agreed on a time and place for the encounter. She heard a car; Michael pulled into the garage to avoid the news crews. He came in the family room carrying a huge plant.

"Oh, Michael! The gardenia's beautiful. The fragrance is heavenly. Thank you, Sweetheart."

"You're very welcome. I know how hard the past few weeks have been. And I ordered dinner. It'll be delivered at seven."

"You're the best!" She watered the plant with care, admiring the glossy, dark green leaves and lovely white blossoms. Tears filled Amelia's eyes. Michael came over and wrapped his arms around her.

"It's OK, Honey. This whole thing is overwhelming. Maybe it's good that you're getting away for a few days. Is Indira going to pick you up at the airport?"

She hugged her husband then retrieved a tissue and dried her eyes. "Yeah, she'll be there. It's a topsy-turvy world right now."

"No kidding." Michael went to the bar cart in the dining room and poured himself a glass of scotch. "Honey, can I get you something?"

"No thanks, I'll wait until dinner arrives. Thanks again for ordering. I'm so not in the mood to cook tonight."

"I'm not either. What do you think will happen with the Russia investigation, now that the head of the FBI is out and the third person to be fired?" he asked as he returned to the family room.

"There's obviously a cover up. Will it lead to impeachment, or 45's resignation? I'm not sure."

"Treasonous collusion with a foreign adversary and knowledge of illegal activity could be charged. Then there's the emoluments clause, and conflicts of interest by him and his family. Filling the swamp with corrupt billionaires. And still the GOP defends T to save their butts, even after he gives classified information to the Russians in the Oval Office!"

"Welcome to the new America. The man-child can't help but inflate his ego by giving an enemy classified info. He did it again with the president of the Philippines. Unfortunately, he's undermined the intelligence community and our allies. He is dangerous."

"He calls it a successful meeting with the Russians, and makes his minions lie for him!"

The ringing doorbell interrupted their conversation. Michael greeted the delivery person and paid for the order as reporters called out questions. Amelia poured herself a glass of wine. Nashville-style hot chicken, ribs, and mac and cheese from their favorite BBQ restaurant were set out on the kitchen table.

"I thought when we won the lottery all our problems would magically disappear," Michael said between mouthfuls of chicken. "But there will always be challenges. I just never imagined we'd have paranormal problems broadcast on the internet."

"It's *fantastic*, not worrying about money anymore," Amelia declared. "You're right about our new concerns. We have The Magician in our lives, but it's not the type of magic we anticipated."

The ribs, chicken, and mac and cheese quickly disappeared.

"When you're in DC for the wedding, I've decided to visit my old boss in Dallas. His cancer has returned, and I don't have a good feeling about it this time."

"I'm glad you're going. Please give him my love. Cancer can strike anyone at any time: rich or poor, Democrat or Republican."

"My only hesitation," Michael began, "was dealing with any political discussions with the Texans."

"I've been thinking of calling it 'The New Great Divide.' People would rather destroy their relationships with family and friends than admit they were wrong."

"But so many people don't believe what's happening is wrong. That's the hard part."

Michael got up and poured two glasses of water to counteract the hot chicken. "How can we build a bridge across the chasm? When the norms of democracy are tossed out the door, and checks and balances in government are tenuous, how do we move forward?"

CHAPTER 24

The Tarot Card

F elicity Henderson, draped in an embroidered kaftan, joined Amelia at the covered picnic table at Peter's Point Beachside Park. The psychic looked just as Amelia imagined she would—wild, curly hair framing a kind face. The women looked skyward as a flock of pelicans swooped overhead and soared southward. Massive white clouds sailed over the ocean as a gentle breeze brought welcome relief from the oppressive heat.

"Hi, Felicity. You look familiar."

"So do you. It's a small island. We must have crossed paths at some point. I'm glad you could meet me today."

"My experiences since my accident have been unnerving. And the media attention is downright disturbing."

"Being 'different' has always been perilous. How many women were murdered or exiled for supposedly being witches? People fear what's unfamiliar, or what they don't understand."

"I've heard that a lot lately."

"It's an explanation, not an excuse. Seeing through another's eyes can give us a new perspective."

Amelia chuckled. "That's what I've been learning since my time on the other side. I've tried to see the world through my spiritual, as well as physical eyes. Understanding subjective versus objective truths."

"We come into the world with a life blueprint. Yours probably included a trip to the spirit world at some point. Once the predetermined event occurs, we have choices to make about how we respond. We can internalize the lessons and act on the new insights, or we can stick our heads in the sand."

"Sometimes the sand looks like a good choice!" Amelia said.

Felicity smiled and took a deck of Tarot cards from her bag. "I inherited my psychic abilities from my mother and grandmother. My gifts have been a part of me since childhood, and I had support growing up. It must be difficult to have them thrust upon you with no understanding of how to handle them."

"That's for sure. Maybe you're right that this is part of my destiny. I've never actually seen Tarot cards before."

After shuffling and fanning the cards, Felicity placed the deck face down on the table. "Please choose one."

Amelia ran her hand over the cards until one felt slightly warm. She pulled it from the deck and handed it to Felicity. The psychic's face betrayed her puzzlement at the card she held. She looked at Amelia.

"Oh my. This is interesting." She turned the card so Amelia could see. It was The Magician. "What does it mean to you?"

Amelia held the card and closed her eyes. In her mind, she swiftly returned to the darkened theater of her previous vision. The VP was under the spotlight in his long, black cape. His face was shadowed by a fedora. Raising his eyes to Amelia, his smarmy grin sent shivers down her spine. She found the courage to call out to him, "What are you trying to tell me?"

"Amelia! Come back. Who were you talking to?"

Shaken and peering around to get her bearings, Amelia dropped the card on the picnic table. "I...it was...the vice president. I didn't mean to say that out loud. I've seen him in a vision before. This time he just creepily smiled at me. He didn't say or do anything. I don't understand what's happening!"

"The Magician card can indicate the intoxication of power. In this case I think it applies to the man in your vision. Do you have any connection to him?"

"No, none at all. All this seems so random. I have no connection to politics whatsoever."

"Well, if I get any insights, I'll let you know. And please email me if you have any questions. Here's my card."

Amelia thanked Felicity and handed her a business card. As Amelia walked to her car, a wave of nausea overtook her and she leaned against the door. Finally, she was able to drive home. When she turned the corner, she noticed the news vans were gone. Her relief was short-lived; she saw a large, black SUV parked in her driveway.

She pulled in beside the vehicle as two men exited the car. They were dressed exactly alike, and Amelia immediately thought of the Men in Black and knew they were from the government. She took a deep breath to calm her racing heart and got out.

"Mrs. Jones? I'm FBI Special Agent Gilchrist, and this is Special Agent Mannford. May we speak with you?"

The men held out their credentials. The afternoon sun was beating down and Amelia felt faint. She seriously needed to sit down.

"Yes, of course. But please come inside, out of this heat."

They entered the house and Amelia went into the kitchen for a glass of water. She signaled for the men to have a seat on the great room sofa. She pulled up a chair and flopped down.

"Oh, sorry, can I get you some water?"

"No thank you, Ma'am," said the short, stocky Mannford.

Amelia looked at the tall, well-built Special Agent Gilchrist. "How can I help you?"

"As you know," Gilchrist began, "we take every threat to the administration seriously."

"I haven't threatened anyone!" Amelia blurted out.

"Oh, sorry Ma'am," Mannford chimed in, "we're not accusing you of anything. We're seeking your assistance."

Amelia jumped up and began to pace. She knew where this conversation was going.

"There's been a credible threat to the vice president of the United States. We've identified a local suspect in the conspiracy. We've also been following the postings of your unusual 'abilities' on the internet. We believe you can help us."

"The Magician," Amelia mumbled to herself.

"Pardon, Ma'am?" said Gilchrist.

"Oh, nothing. What do you want from me?"

"We'd like you to come to our Jacksonville office tomorrow. We're interrogating the suspect. You'd be in a secure room and would not interact directly with him, but view him through a mirror. There's no possible danger to you. Are you able to compel people to tell the truth even if you're not in the same room?"

After taking her seat, Amelia looked from one man to the other. "Gentlemen, I really don't know the answer to that question. This ability is new to me. I don't understand how or when it works. Isn't there any other way to get the information you need?"

"With the White House under investigation by the special counsel, events are moving quickly. We believe the vice president is in imminent danger."

"I don't get it," Amelia said.

"You understand that whatever we speak of today is completely confidential. This is classified information, and you are to tell no one the content of this conversation."

"I understand."

"We have uncovered a plot to assassinate the vice president. There's a group of American citizens who believe that the Speaker of the House is the rightful successor, and should have been chosen as VP. If the president is removed from office, the Speaker is third in line. With the VP eliminated, the Speaker would become president."

"Holy shit!" Amelia jumped up and began to pace again. "I totally disagree with everything that's happened since the election. But I can't stand by if there's going to be an assassination attempt on anyone," she said. "Tell me when and where I should be tomorrow."

"Thank you, Ma'am." Mannford handed her a card with the address of the Jacksonville office. "Ten a.m. will work."

"I didn't know the FBI worked with psychics," Amelia commented.

The agents glanced at one another. "It's highly unusual, to be sure," said Gilchrist. "I had an incredible experience with a man who's an intuitive when I worked in Colorado. He's been involved with over a hundred cases in the US and internationally. My neck is on the line by insisting that we ask for your help."

"Wow, no pressure there!" said Amelia. "I'll show you out."

Michael drove up just as the agents were leaving the driveway. A lump of fear formed in his throat. His concern about his wife's psychic gift expanded tenfold.

CHAPTER 25

Mr. Fry

Michael and Amelia drove across the massive suspension bridge spanning the wide St. John's River. To the east were huge, high-sided vehicle transport ships, called ro-ros because the vehicles rolled on and off the ships. Amelia looked west at the incredible number of containers in the Jacksonville port, waiting to be shipped to other American cities and foreign lands.

They exited the highway and headed to the FBI headquarters. Amelia had told her husband what she could about the meeting without revealing too much. Unlike 45, Amelia did not divulge classified information. The tyrant's disgusting actions with the Russians made her ill. She had more valor and common sense than the person in the highest office in the country.

After passing through security, they were seated in a waiting room. Several minutes later, Special Agent Gilchrist entered, pulled up a chair at the table, and opened a file folder.

"Due to the unusual circumstances, we'll allow you, Mr. Jones, to be included in this meeting. But you must swear to keep all information disclosed here today, strictly confidential."

"I understand, and I swear to keep confidential everything you indicate shouldn't be discussed," said Michael.

Amelia fidgeted with her purse, unable to calm her nerves. She didn't want to be there, but felt it was her civic duty to help. Special

Agent Gilchrist provided Michael with the details he'd shared with Amelia the day before.

"The suspect you'll be viewing today, Mrs. Jones, is Alton Fry. He's been linked to a fanatical wing of the Catholic Church in Florida. He was brought to our attention by a former girlfriend."

"If he's from Florida, how's he connected to the Speaker of the House?" Amelia asked.

"He was an undergrad at the Speaker's college. Mr. Fry was in the same program at Miami University of Ohio, but a year behind. We've been digging into their relationship, and Fry appears to have been obsessed with the Speaker. Their common religion and beliefs were the foundation of a bond that soured over time. Fry's erratic behavior concerned many people around him."

"But how did he become involved in a plot against the vice president?" Michael asked.

"We're still tracking down the sequence of events that led Fry to the organization behind the conspiracy. We believe it started in an alt-right chat room after the 2012 election. There was a group who believed the Democrats stole the election, and the Republican nominee should have been president. They planned on forcing the Mormon out and were convinced that the Speaker would have won in 2016."

"So, what do you want from me?" Amelia said.

"We've received conflicting information about the organization's imminent actions. We need to know what is true and what's a diversion. We'd like you to listen in on the interrogation. You'll be in a secure room; when we give you the signal, you can ask Mr. Fry to tell the truth. I will turn toward the mirror and nod," said Gilchrist.

"Can I be in the room with Amelia?" Michael asked.

"Yes, Mr. Jones."

Michael took Amelia's hand and looked into her eyes. "Are you ready to do this? You don't have to."

"Thanks, Honey, but I need to try. I'm still not sure it will work if I'm not in the same room."

Gilchrist rose. "Good then. There's coffee and pastries on the side table. Help yourself. Someone will come for you when we're ready." He swiftly left the room.

Amelia began to pace as Michael poured two cups of coffee and brought them to the table.

"Thanks, but I don't need any more caffeine. I'm anxious enough. I really hope this works—and I really hope it doesn't. What if I'm successful, and I get hauled in here every time the FBI is stuck? I don't want to do this on a regular basis."

"I don't blame you. I've been worried that the outing of your ability would disrupt our lives, and it has. I know it's not your fault. Others have posted videos, and we've had no control."

Amelia walked over to her husband. He wrapped his arms around her and held her tight. "Thanks, Sweetheart, for your support through all this madness."

"You can always count on me. Now and forever."

Moments later, an FBI agent entered the room. "Mrs. Jones, please come with me."

Amelia and Michael followed the young man into a room with a large mirror. Through the glass they could see Special Agents Gilchrist and Mannford sitting across from a conservatively dressed man with short, grey hair. He appeared average in every way, except for a trapped-animal look in his eyes.

Fry's lawyer was seated beside him, sweating profusely. He was rotund, with what can best be described as a permanent sneer. His expensive shirt was straining at the belly, and his slicked-back hair looked greasy.

"I'm Alice through the looking glass. And down the rabbit hole!" Amelia said softly.

Michael took her hand and gave it a squeeze before letting go. He wasn't sure how else he could support his wife in this moment. The questioning of Fry began, and the Joneses listened intently. The agents described several conspiracies that they'd been aware of, but Fry stonewalled like the new attorney general at the Senate investigation. The perspiring lawyer constantly asserted that his client could not comment.

Agent Gilchrist rose from his chair and started to pace. Fry fidgeted and began scribbling on the paper that had been placed in front of him. Gilchrist looked at the mirror and nodded.

"Mr. Fry, the truth be told," Amelia said aloud and with conviction as a strong vibration went up her spine. Fry suddenly stopped scribbling and gazed intensely at the mirror. With horrified look on his face, he began to mumble. His whole body shook like he'd been given an electric shock. Amelia was confused; she wasn't sure if her ability worked, since she wasn't in the interrogation room.

Then Alton Fry told the truth. He spoke of a group of Miami of Ohio alumni who were determined to see the Speaker in the White House as president. He talked about The Deacons, an alt-right group within the Catholic Church who wanted to see the VP eliminated, and were working with the Miami of Ohio alliance. Next, he raged against fake movies like *Philomena* and *Spotlight* that twisted the facts of church scandals and misled the public. He opined that a few bad apples didn't mean the whole barrel of Catholicism was rotten.

Then he railed against the traitor in the Oval Office who bowed and curtsied to the Saudi King and wouldn't say 'radical Islamic terrorism' when he visited a Muslim country. Alton also indicated that there was a separate plot against the president by another fringe group, and rumors of a conspiracy against Democratic leaders.

The obese lawyer sat in stunned silence with his mouth hanging open. He finally yelled at his client to stop talking. Alton Fry's head dropped to the table.

CHAPTER 26

Free Will

With trepidation, Amelia boarded the plane for Washington, DC. Her mind was still reeling from her adventure at FBI headquarters. She was grateful that Michael had been with her. The scope of the conspiracies revealed by Fry was overwhelming.

The memory of her visions of DC caused her anxiety. Also, she now had a personal connection to the administration in the White House. Never in her wildest dreams could she have imagined the course of recent events.

After landing and collecting her suitcase, she walked outside and saw Indira's lovely, smiling face. Indira's parents had emigrated to the US two months before she was born. In some ways, she still had a foot in India—but in other ways she was a typical American. She was Amelia's boss at her first adult job, and the women had remained close ever since. Indira's husband had passed away three years earlier, and her two children were living in Southern California.

Amelia held back tears of relief as she hugged her friend and mentor. They drove to Indira's house and Amelia settled into the guest room. She then went to the walled garden behind the townhouse, where glorious roses and peonies filled the air with a delightful fragrance. The afternoon sun bathed the garden in warmth.

"So, my dear friend, tell me everything," Indira said.

Without taking a breath, Amelia covered every detail of her life since the accident except for the classified information. When she finished, she felt drained but also renewed by the energy that Indira had been sending her. It was like she'd been through a storm and the sun was shining once again.

"It feels good to tell the story in a coherent way," Amelia added. "It's still hard to believe that it all really happened."

"I agree with Felicity that your life blueprint included a journey to the other side and the emergence of a psychic gift. That you've chosen to embrace this new ability to help others is a testament to your spiritual strength."

"That's one of the things that's been bothering me the most. The soul of the nation seems dark and cold, like the GOP's healthcare plan and budget. The lack of empathy with the less fortunate is terrible. It's like poverty is a crime they think should be punished. The Republican leaders say it's compassionate to cut funding to the elderly, children, disabled, and struggling working poor. That the wealthy taxpayers need compassion too."

Indira sighed and poured two glasses of iced tea. "The journey to enlightenment is not a direct path. Sometimes there are roadblocks and detours. My hope is that this administration is a temporary obstruction in the road. Although there are so many regressive policies that it may be a new dark age in American history. This is very similar to fascism in Germany in the 1930s."

"I'd like your opinion on the state of the union, so to speak. Do you mind if I write your ideas down?" Amelia asked.

"Of course I wouldn't mind."

Amelia went to the guest room and retrieved a journal and pen. She returned to the garden for a discourse on the political reality. She twirled the pen in her hand as she flopped in the chair.

"I remember using my mom's fountain pen when I was a child. I'd dip the tip in the bottle of ink and pull back the lever to fill the reservoir. I'd always make a mess, splattering drops of black ink on the white paper. I have no idea why that memory surfaced."

"Perhaps so you can appreciate the ease of ballpoint pens. And when you use a computer for your compositions, you can effortlessly correct your mistakes. There are benefits to progress," answered Indira.

Amelia laughed. "I guess you're right. My mom always got angry with me for wasting paper. It's incredible how memories from childhood surface unexpectedly. But back to the topic at hand..."

"Well," Indira began, "let's talk about human nature. Many people live in survival mode, just trying to feed their families and secure their future. Any threat to their finances and their way of life is vehemently attacked. This includes the others whom they see as a danger."

"I get that," said Amelia. "People work hard for their money, and some don't want to support others. They're like small children who haven't learned to share. But why are so many people in the deplorable category? The misogyny, racism, Islamophobia, homophobia, xenophobia, and all the rest."

"Free will means that we can choose good or evil, generosity or selfishness, kindness or cruelty. Many people follow what they've been taught by their families, religion, communities, and society in general, and don't think for themselves. They can't be bothered to question the truth about what they've been told. They search for facts that validate their world view," said Indira.

"Blue lies, the kind that people accept if the lies support their tribe view and confirm their beliefs, rational or not. 45 tapped into their fear and anxiety in a masterful way," Amelia added.

"And their frustration. The gridlock in government was more pronounced than ever before. The discord had risen to the surface and was validated by the Tea Party and their success during the elections following the first black president."

"Like the Breitbart followers, they wanted to blow up the system and thought a businessman could do it. He promised to drain the swamp, but he's only added more lobbyists, millionaires, and billionaires to DC. He said in a speech in Iowa that he doesn't want poor people running government agencies. And his supporters don't question it!"

"You're correct, Amelia. The wealthy and powerful want to protect their interests at the expense of the rest of us. They have no plans to actually fix the system, because they don't want the redistribution of their wealth. The oil and gas industry, big pharma, big insurance and healthcare companies, private schools, and private prisons now have the power to move the country backward. Any legislation that restricted them or caused lower profits will probably be overturned. Regression rather than progression."

Amelia continued to record the discussion. She was serious about writing a novel to chronicle this unprecedented time. Indira went into the kitchen and returned with a plate of fruit and lemon pound cake. The women ate the delicacies as they digested the conversation.

"Let's also look at the American character. This country was founded on the pioneering spirit. These types of people created some of America's greatest achievements in science, technology, health, and even the arts. The individualism and adventurousness can be positive. But a narcissistic, aggressive mentality," said Indira, "can be the dark side of the character."

"You're right. Americans have made advancements in so many fields. On the flip side, the Wild West attracted fierce and often violent people. Michael's ancestors lived in Pennsylvania, but moved to Canada as United Empire Loyalists because they didn't want to fight in the Revolutionary War. Canada was opened up in a civilized way, with the Mounties leading the trek west."

"Exactly. Pacifists left the country, and the glorification of the 'cult of the individual' became the norm here long before social media. Narcissism is venerated. Entertainers are exalted, and the line between fantasy and reality is blurred."

Amelia thought about what her friend had said. "I've read that when you go to a movie there's a suspension of belief. You agree to accept a fictional world as real, at least for as long as the movie lasts. Some citizens have accepted 45's insane worldview as real. Mexico will pay for the wall. It doesn't matter that his decisions are influenced by foreign money. His nepotism is justified. It's OK if millions of people will lose health care because people will have more 'choice' and only the sick, elderly, and those with pre-existing conditions will be hurt. People he definitely doesn't care about."

"The American dream is actually an American fantasy," Indira added. "Some have gone from rags to riches, and their success feeds the national psyche. People say, 'I don't want taxes raised on the rich because maybe someday I'm going to be rich too.' The possibility of upward mobility is greater in other countries, even your home country of Canada. Many

Americans believe they're better than others simply because they were born here. It blinds people to reality."

Amelia continued to jot down ideas as they came to her. "It reminds me of survival of the fittest. Leave the weak behind or eradicate them, like Hitler did when he sterilized and even murdered the handicapped."

Indira sighed. "That's the psychopath's way—they have no shame, remorse, or compassion. With a psychopathic narcissist in control, what else should we expect?"

"The disgusting butt-kissing the Cabinet did at their first meeting with the king shows that clearly. Yet there are millions of amazing, kind, compassionate people in the country. How do we get a government that exalts the best in humanity?"

"That is something you need to keep in mind. Continue to meditate and journal about the situation. You have an important role in the narrative, although it may not be clear to you yet," Indira stated. "Follow the messages from your soul."

CHAPTER 27

Human Nature

The sound of thunder and flashes of lightening interrupted the exchange of ideas. The women gathered the glasses and remains of the cake and brought them to the kitchen. Settling into the comfortable, antique-filled living room, they continued their conversation.

"Speaking of the soul, what about the spiritual aspect of all this?" Amelia questioned. "I feel my spirit has been assaulted."

"My sentiments exactly."

As the darkness grew, Indira turned on two Tiffany lamps. Amelia felt safe in the cozy room, and more relaxed than she'd been in a long time.

Amelia continued. "The concept that religion is the opium of the masses, and that social media could also be seen as the opium of the masses, both make sense to me. Many would rather be told what to believe and how to buy their way into heaven. They pick and choose passages in the Bible that defend their beliefs and they ignore the rest."

Indira went to an overstuffed shelf and picked out a book. She opened it to a dog-eared page.

"I agree," said Indira. "How many have used religion to justify all sorts of atrocities, including murder? The shadow side of religion is ever present. It reminds me of what Deepak Chopra wrote about the shadow in this book: 'If authority figures are present to actively incite bad behavior and promise a lack of punishment, the shadow surfaces all the more easily.'"

"Did he write that recently?" Amelia asked.

"No, many years ago. But it applies to what happened during and since the 2016 election. He also wrote, 'The absence of law and order amplifies the effect, as does being given permission to behave beyond normal morality.'"

"Wow, it's like a blueprint for the GOP's campaign. The tyrant incited violence at his rallies, and promised to provide legal defense for the knuckle draggers who committed these crimes."

"Chopra believes that humanity created the dark side and we have the power to uncreate it. I agree, but I'm not certain how we attain this change in the human character."

"People also want to constantly be entertained, and that brings us back to social media," said Amelia. "Critical thinking about their lives is too mentally challenging. Show me puppies and kittens, and don't ask me to contemplate the nature of existence. The anonymity provided gives people the freedom to be cruel."

"This is not a spiritually mature society. The concept promoted by evangelicals, to be 'born again,' is part of the problem. If people are born again, then they are like children that can be manipulated by the religious leaders. The religious hierarchy doesn't want mature, self-actualized members—they want compliant children who are willing to be led, and who will financially support them."

"I hadn't thought of it in those terms. Like the terms 'father' and 'mother superior' in the Catholic Church openly suggest the hierarchy. They want obedience," said Amelia.

"Yes, and the worshipers follow blindly and unquestioningly."

"It's startling how right-wing Christians have turned a blind eye to the fact that the emperor shares none of their purported values. He's an adulterer, a sexual predator, and a pathological liar; he cheats his way through life. He's even funneled money meant for children's cancer research into his own pocket! How is *that* following the teachings of Jesus?"

"Christ never demanded tithing," said Indira. "He didn't wear gold- and jewel-encrusted vestments. He didn't insist that enormous cathedrals be built in his honor. None of the great spiritual leaders surrounded themselves with luxuries. It's their followers who usurped the teachers' messages for their personal gain. The Knights Templar began as defenders of pilgrims to the holy land and ended up as powerful, warring, wealthy men. They were exempt from local laws, and only obedient to the pope."

Amelia chuckled. "I can't see how that could go wrong! What do they say about absolute power corrupting absolutely?"

"It was interesting to see Pope Francis's first meeting with 45. The fact that the pope gave the president a copy of his book on climate change was priceless."

"Little pretense there. During the first part of 45's trip abroad, his rhetoric was devoid of his obnoxious ranting. His handlers prayed he'd stick to the script. And his wife prayed he'd stop touching her. Then, against the advice of his cabinet, he pulled out of the Paris Climate Agreement. Jeez!"

"Getting back to spirituality, many believed the 21st century would bring a new age of enlightenment," Indira began. "The social progress was expected to continue. We had overcome so much inequality that the future looked bright. The Age of Aquarius had created a space for personal spiritual growth. People were told that their thoughts created things, and that they could attract whatever they wanted, including relationships and wealth."

"I know. I've explored several New Age teachings. I can't tell you how many books I've read and courses I've taken. Some wonderful things have manifested in my life, but the bubble burst after the election."

"Yes, we have to temper our beliefs in our individual power with the fact that we co-create this world with everyone else on the planet. There is a limit to what we can physically control."

"I sometimes wonder if the world would be a better place without religion. John Lennon said something about that," Amelia added.

"I believe that people who've lived many lifetimes and are spiritually advanced no longer need the dogma and rules of organized religion. But those who are new to the earth plane need the guidance. They also need a reminder that we are essentially spiritual beings."

"I understand. But how do we move forward when religion and politics divide us?"

"That's the million-dollar question, my friend. And what we've talked about tonight is a simplification of religion and human nature. Some think that life is random. I believe we come into the world by choice. On an astral level we know that nature and human beings can be magnificent and terrible."

Amelia's cell phone vibrated in her pocket. There was a text message from Michael, who was in Dallas visiting his ill ex-boss.

"Indira, would you please turn on the TV?"

Indira picked up the remote and turned to a news station. There was report about the Republican Montana nominee for Congress who attacked a reporter. He body-slammed the young man after being questioned about the new healthcare plan. Both women were shocked by the violence and the lies that came from the GOP party after the incident.

"We were just talking about the aggressive, even violent character of many Americans. There will be a lot of people who were incited to hate the media by the orange one's campaign against the press. Too many will see this behavior as acceptable," Amelia commented.

"And then again, dear Amelia, thousands of people are beginning to find their voice. They're not focusing on their 'silo' or individual issues, but are looking toward forming alliances with other assaulted groups to defend the rights of all. Even politicians and lawyers are contributing to a wave of resistance. Our spirits can be crushed by fascism, or they can be elevated by the winds of loving change."

"It's reaching the consciences of Independents and moderate Republicans who can join with us. Will they be the wind beneath our wings?" Amelia questioned.

CHAPTER 28

Unexpected Guest

The following morning, Lyla arrived at Indira's to pick up Amelia. The plan was to tour the city before checking into the hotel in Georgetown where the wedding would take place. The three women were having coffee in the fragrant garden when Amelia received a phone call.

"Katrina. How are you doing?"

"He found me, Amelia! I'm on the run again."

"Oh my God! What happened?"

Katrina choked back tears. "It's my fault. I gave the Philly address to a co-worker so she could mail my paycheck. I told her not to tell anyone where I was, but Connor tricked her into telling him."

"I'm so sorry. Where are you now?"

"Driving south on 95 just north of DC. Conner came when I was out, and Marilyn texted me to stay away from the house. Fortunately, I always packed my suitcase and had it with me."

"Come to my friend Indira's house in Reston, Virginia. You're not too far from here. I'll text you the address."

Amelia looked over at Indira, who nodded. These women would never turn away a person in need.

"It's discouraging that the Florida police couldn't identify a possible victim. They even checked with the Georgia cops, because the St. Mary's River is the border between the two states."

"Maybe the crime happened in a different state," Indira said. "I know there's a St. Mary's River in Maryland. I've been to the state park on the river."

"I hadn't thought of that. When Katrina gets here she can call the Jacksonville police and see if they'll be able to follow up with Maryland. And if that doesn't pan out, they should search other rivers with the same name."

"I'll make more coffee. Can I get you anything else?"

"I'm good," Lyla answered.

Amelia shook her head no. "Sorry to drag you and Indira into this. I pray Connor isn't following her. I'm glad I filled you both in on Katrina's situation."

"Crazy how things have been altered since I pulled you out of the ocean. Who could have imagined that a bonk on the head would cause major changes in your life?"

A short time later, Katrina rang the doorbell. Indira brought her to the garden, where Amelia and Lyla were waiting.

"I'm sorry about all this, Amelia. You've been so helpful, and now I'm causing more trouble," Katrina said as she dropped into a chair.

"It's OK. Marilyn just texted that Connor hasn't shown up again. He has no idea where you went."

Katrina sheepishly said, "But like an idiot I mentioned your name to my co-worker. And she told Connor that you'd helped me."

Amelia was shocked at the confession. "Oh no! It won't be hard for him to find out where we live on the island. I'm glad Michael's in Dallas right now."

Covering her face with her hands, Katrina began to sob. "I can't handle any more of this! I'm ashamed and scared."

Indira began, "My dear girl, no one is ever prepared for a situation such as this. Amelia and I had the idea that your impression of the victim being disposed of in St. Mary's River could be correct, but in a different state. I know there's one in Maryland."

Katrina looked up through tear-filled eyes. "I hadn't thought of that!"

"Why don't you call your contact in the Jacksonville police department, and see if they can check with other states?" said Amelia.

"I guess they can't bring him in for questioning based on a psychic impression," added Lyla. "I wonder if he'll head back to Florida."

"Who knows?" Katrina said as she took a tissue from her purse and dried her tears. "This whole thing sucks. I'll call the Jax police right now."

"You're welcome to stay with me as long as you need to," Indira said and smiled warmly at the young woman.

Katrina smiled at her host, then grabbed her phone and went into the house to make the call.

"Do you want to stay here or tour the city?" Lyla asked Amelia.

"Please don't change your plans. Katrina can remain here with me until she decides what to do next," said Indira.

"If you wouldn't mind," Amelia began. "I don't think he was able to follow her, so you should be safe."

"We'll be fine. Enjoy your tour of the nation's capital."

Amelia packed her suitcase and joined Lyla in the rented car. They merged into the traffic slowly making its way into DC and parked near Pennsylvania Avenue. Amelia's heart pounded as they walked in front of the White House. She nervously watched every white van that passed.

After they left the area and hopped on a trolley tour, Amelia finally relaxed and enjoyed the day. Her terrible vision of being abducted hadn't come true.

CHAPTER 29

Little Talbot Island

A melia and Lyla boarded the plane bound for Jacksonville. They were overjoyed that the wedding had been a wonderful event. Lyla reveled in the time spent with her daughter, Annabelle. At the wedding, it was obvious that the bride and groom were perfectly matched, and the guests left feeling uplifted by the celebration.

The women were also happy they were heading home. The constant worry that one or both of them would be abducted while they were in DC preyed on their minds. Settling into their seats, they reviewed the events of the past few days. Katrina had called as they were driving to the airport and updated Amelia on the Connor situation.

The police were investigating the possibility that the victim was from another part of the country. Katrina was safe and staying with Indira for the foreseeable future, and Marilyn hadn't seen or heard from Connor. Amelia had told Michael to be careful when he returned from Dallas. He was upset that Katrina had mentioned Amelia's name and that they could be in danger.

After picking up their cars at the Jacksonville airport parking lot, they drove north on Highway 95 to the Amelia Island exit. Each year the traffic was heavier, as more people discovered this incredible part of Florida and made it their home. Locals complained every time the island was promoted in travel magazines.

They waved goodbye as Amelia turned right at the first stop light over the bridge. Michael was sitting on the front porch when she pulled into the driveway. She gulped, fearing something was wrong. She hopped out of the car and rushed to her husband.

"Are you OK?"

"Fine, Honey. Why?"

Amelia exhaled. "When I saw you on the porch, I thought something was wrong inside the house. Like someone had broken in."

Michael hugged his wife. "You do have wild ideas. I thought we'd go for a hike on Little Talbot Island after you get unpacked. You can tell me all about the wedding and Katrina, and I can fill you in on Texas."

They drove to the south end of the island and crossed the bridge, watching as dozens of people dropped their lines into the river on the separate fishing bridge. They continued to the state park on Little Talbot, paid the entrance fee, and picked up a map of the four-mile trail around the island. After they applied bug spray and sunscreen they set out into the maritime hammock.

"Thank goodness the news crews have decided we aren't worth staking out any more," Amelia said. "Since I'm not on social media, it's been nice and quiet. Changing my phone number has helped, too."

"Did Katrina give you the name of her police contact?"

"Yeah, and she's asked him to follow up with us when they know more about Connor and his whereabouts. And if they find a possible victim."

"I'm surprised we haven't heard from the FBI about Fry."

"Me too," Amelia agreed. "It's unsettling to imagine what that crazy group might do."

The wildlife was checking out the visitors as they strolled along. An armadillo scurried over the path as a snake slithered in the opposite direction. Various birds cried out from the live oaks and palmettos. They spotted the rough tail of an alligator slipping into a creek. It was a while before either of the Joneses began their stories.

"I love attending weddings where the families just mesh. Lyla's niece and new husband looked radiant; they reminded me what pure joy looks like."

Michael took her hand and gave it a quick kiss before he released it. "I remember how joyous our wedding was. And through all the ups and downs, it's still a pleasure sharing my life with you."

Unexpectedly, Amelia blushed. "We're so fortunate to have this amazing life and our wonderful children. And hopefully there are more adventures in our future."

Michael laughed. "Honey, haven't you had enough adventures lately?"

"You're right! Maybe I should say more healthy, happy, calm years in our future. So, tell me about your Texas experience."

"Well, Howard's doing better, but he only has a few months at most. He's making peace with all the people he's hurt in the past. I'm glad I could spend some time with him as someone he'd helped, not hurt."

Amelia said, "It's interesting how people gain clarity when facing death. I'm happy he's making amends, and connecting with those he assisted in the past. How's his wife doing?"

"Wife number three is brave and supportive. He's talked to his other wives, and has done his best to smooth the waters. Imminent death can make people more forgiving."

"What about his political views? As I recall, he supported the alt-right."

"Sadly, his views on politics haven't changed. I like the guy, but he's definitely one of the deplorables. He still has intense animosity toward immigrants and gays. It's mind-boggling how conditional his compassion is."

"What a shame he'll leave this world dragging all that baggage with him. Or like Marley's ghost, he'll be carrying the heavy chains of hatred."

"A softening of his heart isn't likely to happen. Unless three spirits visit him in the night and show him the error of his ways," said Michael. "Howard justifies or denies all the lies. He defends alternative facts, and attacks the 'weak liberals' who support universal healthcare. He still believes it's a privilege for those who work and not a right for all."

"If he didn't have healthcare all these years to fight the cancer I bet he'd have a different opinion."

"So, Amelia, where do we go from here? How do we build that bridge we've been talking about? If even the prospect of death doesn't change someone's mind, what does the future look like?"

Amelia knew the questions weren't rhetorical, but she didn't have any answers. They walked in silence for a long while as they mulled over the most pressing concerns of the time. They jumped when a large, prehistoric-looking gator slid into the marshes beside the path.

"Wow! I hope none of those guys make their way to the pond behind our house. There are a lot of small dogs in the neighborhood," said Amelia.

"Small children, too! I know the county removes alligators from residential ponds, but I still don't want one on the lanai or breaking through the screen door. I meant to ask you if you used your special abilities when you were in DC."

"No, I was careful not to ask people personal questions, and never asked anyone to tell the truth. Now every comment or question has to go through a mental screening before I speak. It's exhausting when I'm in a crowd."

"Do you think you'll ever go back to normal?"

"I hadn't thought about that. I've just accepted this as the way my life is now."

CHAPTER 30

New Normal

Amelia got off the phone with the Jacksonville police. They'd identified a young woman who went missing in Maryland six years earlier. Eighteen-year-old Abigail Santos disappeared after leaving a friend's house around midnight. She was only two blocks from home when she vanished without a trace. The search was extensive, but hundreds of tips had resulted in no credible leads. As with all unsolved disappearances, it was heartbreaking for her family.

Michael strolled into the great room and Amelia joined him on the big, comfy sofa. They each had their favorite spot on the couch.

"The Jax police have a lead on a possible victim. A young woman named Abigail disappeared six years ago near the St. Mary's River in Maryland. They're looking for Connor now to question him."

"Great! That's progress. I guess Katrina was onto something when she said Abby or Annie."

"I wonder if the police will ask me to be there, if and when they question him. This new normal is not what I expected. I don't want to be involved with every missing person case!"

"You'll have to take it case by case, Honey. Say yes when you want to and no if the situation feels dangerous. I didn't expect to ever say this, but trust your spidey sense."

Amelia smiled. She never thought she'd hear her husband suggest she use her intuitive skills, but these were unusual times.

"I wish we'd hear something about Fry's organization. That was a crazy story he told. I had no idea there was a chapter of the Catholic group Opus Dei in Jacksonville. Every time I think of it I see the priest in *The Da Vinci Code* flagellating himself. Yuck."

"I'm sure it's rare, but lashing yourself is nuts," Michael said. "What worries me is your name being leaked to the public. What if someone in the FBI reveals that you were the one able to break this assassination plot?"

Amelia gasped. That scenario hadn't crossed her mind. "Yeah, with all the leaks in the intelligence community, I guess it's possible. That thought won't help me sleep tonight."

"Sorry, but it's something we have to consider. They still have Fry in custody. But what if he finds out why he spilled the beans and informs one of the others in his organization? Make sure you set the alarm when I leave for Tampa in the morning."

"You don't have to remind me!"

The following day, Michael left for his meeting and Amelia went back to her journal. She decided it was time to start entering her thoughts into a computer file. She made a pot of coffee, set up her laptop on the kitchen table, and set to work. She received a text from the Jacksonville police saying there was an APB out on Connor Stewart. He hadn't been to his job as a motorcycle mechanic, or been seen at his apartment building, for several days.

Her cell phone rang in the bedroom and she rushed to answer it. Since she'd changed her number, she knew it could only be someone close to her.

"Hey, Momma. How ya doin'?"

"Ben, it's so good to hear from you! Your dad just left for Tampa, and I'm putting down my thoughts about what's been going on. The wedding in DC was wonderful. I'm glad I went. The police are making progress on Katrina's case, so that's positive. How's work going?"

"That's what I'm calling about. I might have an opportunity to work in Toronto for a couple of years. Back to the homeland! What's your take?"

"Wow! That would be a great opportunity, since you're a plane ride from here anyway. Very cool! Having international experience is always good for your career. When will you know?"

"Well, they've actually offered me the position, but there are some details to work out. I won't make a commitment until I'm sure it's the right job for me."

"You'd make your old mom happy if you were a Toronto Maple Leafs fan. I'm the only one in the family who likes that hockey team the best."

Ben laughed. "Well, it's possible. The Leafs are better now than they've been in decades. I'll let you know if the job works out. Love you."

"Love you, too."

Amelia went back to her computer and opened a new Word document. She typed in Alton Fry and centered the name, then began to list the details of the situation and his confession.

Alton Fry was a member of The Deacons, a splinter group of Opus Dei. Their mission was to place as many Catholics in positions of power as possible. They anticipated that the president would leave office before his full term, one way or another. With the VP eliminated, the Speaker of the House would be the president; with the help of the GOP, they would place Catholicism at the forefront of legislation. With the presidency, Senate, and House all under Republican control, this was the best time to achieve their agenda. They'd witnessed the extensive power that a sitting president has when one party is in complete control.

They viewed the vice president as a traitor because he'd been raised as a Catholic and became an evangelical Christian when he attended university. He'd become a vocal advocate for the religious right as a radio and television talk show host before he became active in Indiana politics. He was proud to say he was "a Christian, a conservative, and a Republican, in that order."

He was one of the hypocritical Tea Party members, now called the Freedom Caucus, who attacked the Democratic nominee for using a private email server when he himself had used a private server for government business as Governor of Indiana.

The Deacons justified the VP's assassination because of his betrayal of his faith—a sacrificial lamb. There were members of the Secret Service who were involved with the group, and willing to participate in the removal of the vice president.

Unfortunately, Fry didn't have the names of possible assassins but he did divulge the name of a contact in the capital who previously worked for the Secret Service. During the interrogation, Fry had gone on a tirade against the moral corruption of 45 and the country as a whole. Then he finally clammed up and dropped his head on the table.

Amelia finished typing, rose from the table, and walked outside. She looked up at the sky through the waiving palm trees and called out, "Dear Lord! How did I get involved in this insanity?"

The ducks in the pond flew off in a panic at the sound of a crazy lady yelling at the sky. She gazed across the water and saw someone waving at her. It was Drew, the creepy orderly. He was at the same house where she and the kids had seen someone taking their photo. She waved back and went inside.

CHAPTER 31

The Finalists

The members of the KNC—the Knights of the New Crusade—were speaking on secure lines about their progress. Each knew secrets about the other members that would ensure no one would betray the cause. The fear of exposure of the truth was what kept them together. After several weeks of research, they'd narrowed the field of Democratic candidates to one woman and two men.

"So, do we hire out or do this ourselves?" asked Dr. Gabriel. "I—I don't know if I can pull the trigger, so to speak."

"I want to keep this in our hands, if possible. Another layer of involvement could make us vulnerable," said Father Rathbone. "I've just heard of a splinter group within Opus Dei that could cause a problem. These idiots want to get rid of the VP even before anything happens to remove the president from office."

Josh Miller chuckled. "Guessin' there's a lot of conspiracies out there. You'd think it would be the crazies on the left wantin' to off the guys in the White House. The Feds must be chasin' their tails figurin' out which threats are real. Oh, mercy. I love all this mayhem!"

"Let's get back to the finalists," the priest said, exasperated. He hated having to trust outsiders, but he wanted to protect the Catholic Church and Opus Dei from any involvement. An American cardinal had already reprimanded Henry for some of his actions. His desire to move the Church back to its core beliefs was an ever-present obsession. His efforts were penance for his weakness of the flesh.

"The female senator from California, the young congressman from Massachusetts, and the governor from Virginia. From this point on their code names are the State Attorney General, the Marine, and the Governor," Dr. Gabriel stated. "These are leading Democratic nominees for 2020. The Marine can appeal to the military, centrists, and millennials. The Governor can attract middle-aged white men and the South."

"And the State A.G. would bring out the ethnic and women's vote," added Father Rathbone. "The elimination of these candidates and the intimidation of the rest of the field will lead us to victory."

The conspirators were silent for a few moments, taking in the weight of what they were proposing. The assassination of political figures was a radical measure to achieve their ends.

Reverend Josh Miller had his own vices. He'd been a gambler since his youth, and had embezzled money from the LCMS, the Lutheran Church-Missouri Synod. This fact had slipped out at the first meeting of the Knights, while they were at the Hotel Del Coronado in San Diego. The reverend would use the success of the KNC's actions if his theft were discovered by the Synod. The leaders of his church would have to forgive him if his actions kept the Republicans in power.

Miller's father had gambled and his vice left their family in ruins. Yet this wasn't enough to prevent Josh from following the same path. He'd convinced himself that he was in control of his addiction—but like most addicts, he definitely was not. He'd become a regular at the casino on the Missouri River.

"Are you gentlemen on board? Once the boulder starts rollin' down the mountain, it can't be stopped," Miller said.

"I'm in," the good priest answered.

"Count me in, too," added the doctor. Dr. Gabriel had his demons. At Freedom University, he led the attack on the LGBTQ community. Yet, he was in love with a male associate professor. Gabriel's wife and children had no idea of his double life. His internal guilt about his same-sex attraction had caused depression in his youth. Eventually, he turned his shame outward and attacked those in the gay community. He wasn't the first evangelical Christian Republican to do so. Nor would he be the last.

All three men knew of the others' sins.

CHAPTER 32

Twilight Zone

Amelia contacted the Sassy Seekers for an emergency meeting on Face-Time. Lyla arrived an hour later, and they greeted the women in Boston together.

Barbara's face filled the computer screen. "Amelia, what's up?"

"I want to fill you in as best I can on an assassination plot against someone in the White House."

The women gasped in unison. Amelia took a deep breath and began her story, withholding only the specific information the FBI agents had told her was confidential. She left out the name of the target, the suspect, and the organization, but discussed the overall details.

"Even though I wasn't in the room, I was able to make him tell the truth. My fear is that somehow my name will get out. And I'm worried that every time the FBI can't solve a crime, they'll haul me in to help. Most of the FBI don't believe in psychics, but this one agent absolutely does."

"This is unbelievable!" said Angie. "We're living in the *Twilight Zone*. That moron has pulled us out of the Paris Climate Agreement, and Catholic extremists are planning assassinations. What the hell is going on?"

"How did this nightmare happen?" asked Emily.

"It comes down to money and the abuse of power. Since Reagan's trickle-down economics, there's been a growing gap between the haves and the have-nots. The middle class has been shrinking, and massive wealth at the top puts power in fewer hands. A corporate coup d'état," said Barbara.

"This has come at a time when most people haven't wanted to get involved in politics."

"You're right," Lyla said. "When only half of eligible voters make it to the polls, it's a sad state."

"Were the FBI agents able to apprehend the conspirators?" asked Emily.

"I don't know. They haven't kept me informed, but I'm assuming no news is good news. I doubt this will be released to the media, so please everyone, keep this confidential."

The women agreed to remain silent about the plot. They all tried to comfort Amelia and assure her everything would be all right.

"You wonder why they don't use a lie detector machine," said Emily.

Lyla answered, "Maybe it's because the results aren't always accepted in court. Outright confessions in the suspect's own words are much better."

"And I'm not sure about truth serums—how they work or what's admissible," added Barbara.

Finally, they said goodbye and Amelia turned off the computer.

"Now that you're in your personal *Twilight Zone*, how do you feel?" Lyla asked as they went out to the lanai. They walked to the edge of the still pond and sat in the lounge chairs. "Six degrees of separation between me and the White House have been reduced to two. I've interacted with the suspect, and know who the target is. I'm so grateful nothing happened while we were in DC."

"I'm worried," Lyla began. "You're involved with a murder plot *and* with an actual murder. Have you heard from the Jacksonville police about Connor Stewart?"

"Not yet. Katrina is still in Virginia. She's afraid she's going to lose her job, but she's more afraid of losing her life. Maybe Michael can help her if she has to find something new."

"In this current political world, I've been exploring the human psyche even more. I was always studying my students in my teaching days. I guess I'm fascinated by what makes us tick."

"Why did you choose middle school? It's such a challenging age," said Amelia.

Lyla sighed. "I realized how difficult that stage of life could be. In a way it's the end of innocence and childhood, but also the blossoming of the adult personality. It reminds me a butterfly emerging from a chrysalis, out and aware but not yet able to open its wings."

"Oh, look! A swarm of yellow butterflies. Perfect timing."

They watched as the yellow insects swirled in unison. An egret took to flight as a blue heron took its place on the pond.

"The fascinating part is seeing 45 act like a petulant fifth grader," said Lyla. "He's the worst type of child—a bully, vindictive and impulsive. And he has the nuclear codes! His tweets are exasperating, but provide insight into his thought processes. They unequivocally demonstrate that he mentally and emotionally never left middle school—if he even made it that far."

"Hopefully the tweets will be considered official statements of the president. They're probably going to be used in the trials against him for his violation of the emoluments clause and obstruction of justice. Oh, I printed out the topics that the orange one has lied about up until recently. It was a list in the Toronto Star newspaper—two hundred ninety-four lies since he took office, and more every day."

Amelia handed her friend the printout.

"Air traffic control; Barack Obama; Brexit; Canada; China; crime; Democrats; exaggeration; healthcare; Hillary Clinton; his inauguration; immigration; jobs; Mexico; NATO; North Korea; oil and coal; Paris Climate Accord; pipelines; promises; religion; Russian ties; sexual assault allegations; tax reform; terrorism; the Middle East; the Trump White House; the courts; the economy; the election; the environment; the media; the military; trade; Twitter; US intelligence; voter Fraud..."

"What a strange time!" Amelia exclaimed. "And he really does seem senile when he walks off a plane and doesn't see a huge black limo right in front of his nose. It's frightening that he has the codes!"

"We don't know how this political drama will end. He could certainly be charged with perjury when he's out of office. And it's bizarre to know that you have a personal connection to it, my friend!"

CHAPTER 33

Abby

Katrina returned to Jacksonville Beach. She'd called her coworker and found out that her boss had threatened to fire her if she didn't come in immediately. Since she was afraid to go to her apartment, she went to a childhood friend's house. She notified the police of her return to work, and they had assured her they were looking for Connor Stewart. They'd assumed he'd left the area. She'd told Indira that she was going to stay with a friend but not that she was returning to Florida.

On the second day after she got back, Katrina left her office and headed for lunch at a restaurant two blocks away. As she rounded the corner, a four-door pickup truck with South Carolina plates pulled up beside her. Stewart jumped out, grabbed her, and pressed a chloroform-laced cloth over her nose and mouth. He threw her into the back seat and hopped in the front.

He'd only driven a few blocks when sirens began wailing. Local marked police cars and unmarked vehicles blocked his way. Stewart screeched to a stop as gun-bearing police surrounded the vehicle. He put up his hands and got out of the car. He was handcuffed and placed in the back of a police cruiser.

Katrina slowly regained consciousness, as a police officer helped her out of the truck. An ambulance drove up at that moment, and paramedics came rushing over and guided her to the vehicle. They placed an oxygen mask over her mouth and nose. She breathed deeply several times, then removed the mask.

"We'll take you to the hospital for a thorough check," said a paramedic.

"I'm fine, really I'm OK," Katrina mumbled, shaking her head. She had remembered she'd have to pay for the ambulance ride. It wasn't covered under her healthcare plan. "No, I'm all right. I want to talk to the police."

With a slight wobble, Katrina approached an officer she recognized from the police station. "Is it him? Is it Connor?"

"Yes," Officer Anson said. "We've been following you. It was our best chance of drawing Stewart out. They found his car in South Carolina, and we assumed he'd found another vehicle. It's a good thing you informed us you'd be back at work."

Another officer escorted Katrina to her office. Her boss, Patrick, came running over and the officer explained what had occurred. Patrick apologized for threatening to fire her. Katrina assured him it was fine; in the end it was better that Stewart had been drawn out and was now in custody.

Later that evening, Katrina returned to her apartment after making a statement at the police department. She called Amelia to give her an update.

"Thanks for everything, Amelia. I never meant to put you in danger. Sorry my coworker mentioned you'd helped me."

"It's OK. We can't control everything and everyone. Thankfully Connor is locked up now. Did they question him about Abby Santos's disappearance?"

"Yeah, and he denied knowing anything about it."

"Did you tell the Jax police about me?" Amelia asked.

There was silence on the other end of the phone. Amelia took a deep breath and waited for a reply.

"Yes, I did."

"Do you think they'll want me to help?"

"I don't know. I'm so sorry about all this!"

"It's fine, Katrina. Let me know if there's more news."

Amelia hung up the phone and walked out the front door to watch the sun set behind the trees. The sky was filled with orange and rose-colored clouds. The beauty of the evening sky always filled her heart with joy. But tonight, her happiness was tinged with anxiety. *Will I be called in to get Connor to confess?*

By 8:00 the following morning, her question was answered. Hoping for quick closure on the case, Officer Anson called and requested her assistance that afternoon. Amelia walked into the office and Michael looked up from his desk.

"What's up?"

"I just heard from the Jax police. They want me to come in today and 'do my thing' to make Connor Stewart confess."

"I'm not surprised. What are you going to do?"

"I want this all to be over, so I'm going to try. I have no idea if I still have the 'gift,' but Stewart can't be released back into society."

"Do you want me to come with you?" Michael asked.

"No, it's OK, Honey. I can do this on my own. Thanks anyway."

Amelia arrived at the Jacksonville police station shortly after noon. As before, she was led into a room with a one-way mirror and an interrogation room on the other side of the glass. Stewart was brought inside and his handcuffs were removed. He chugged a bottle of water that had been placed on the table. A few minutes later, his disheveled lawyer rushed in. He was short and skinny, with a handlebar mustache, and wearing cowboy boots.

Amelia noticed colors swirling around Connor's head and like before, they were muted shades of muddy brown with swirls of bright red. She assumed the red indicated anger.

Two officers grilled him about his attempted abduction of Katrina. He said it was a personal matter about a stolen motorcycle, and he knew that she was involved in the crime. Then they questioned him about the disappearance of Abigail Santos. He insisted he had no knowledge of anyone by that name. Officer Anson provided details of the case, but got nowhere with the suspect.

His inept lawyer kept butting in, but added nothing to the conversation. Stewart chugged bottled water and fidgeted with the papers in front of him.

Almost twenty minutes later, the officer stood up and paced the room. He turned toward the mirror and nodded. Amelia saw her sign. A vibration went up her spine and she said loud and clear, "Connor Stewart, the truth be told."

Connor jumped in his seat like he'd been given an electric shock. He glanced around nervously. Beads of sweat appeared on his forehead as he strained to keep quiet. Then he began his confession of the abduction, rape, and murder of Abby Santos.

CHAPTER 34

Rookies

Amelia sipped lemonade as she sat in the chair on the front porch. Stewart's disturbing confession had taken its toll on her emotional well-being. She wished she could erase his description of the crime from her memory. *At least Abby's family will have some closure.*

Her neighbor Hailey came by, followed by her girls on their bikes.

"Hi, Amelia, how are you? You look rather grim."

Amelia smiled, hoping her grin covered the anguish she was feeling. "Hello, Hailey. I haven't seen you for a while. I'm doing all right."

Hailey walked up and sat in the empty chair. "Is it about your...special ability?"

"I guess you could say that. I've been working with the police on a couple of cases."

"Good for you. I know it can't be easy. They'd only ask you if it was really serious. What else have you been up to?"

"I've decided to start writing about my experiences: maybe a short story or a novel. I'm going to the Writers by the Sea meeting tomorrow. Maybe they can inspire me to get started."

The girls rode their bikes up and down the street while their mother talked to Amelia. They passed Drew, who was walking his dachshund toward the Joneses' house. He joined the women on the front porch.

"Hi, Mrs. Jones. How've you been? I heard you talk about writing."

"Hi, Drew. I've had some unusual experiences since my accident, as you know. I've thought about putting it all down on paper. I'm joining the local writers' group."

"Do people still read paper books?" Drew asked.

Amelia laughed. "I do! But I'll use a computer to write my story."

"Are you working full time at the hospital, Drew?" Hailey questioned.

"Yeah, and I'm also taking photos for an online and print magazine. My friend Gerry's a journalist; he got me the gig. Oh, Mrs. Jones, I told Gerry about you, and he'd like an interview."

"No, I don't think so. I don't want any more news vans in front of the house."

"OK, but let me know if you change your mind." Drew tugged at the dog's leash and they sauntered away.

"He creeps me out," Hailey whispered. "I don't want to be mean, but there's something unnerving about that guy."

"I agree. He was taking photos of the kids and me after I got home from the hospital. I don't trust him."

"I don't either. Oh, I have a Master of Fine Arts degree. If you'd like me to edit your stories, I'd be happy to help."

"Thanks, Hailey. I'll keep that in mind. I've been reading a couple of books on how to write a novel, and they've given me a foundation."

"Well, stay strong. I'd better get these two home. See you later."

Hailey and her daughters left, and Amelia walked around the house to the backyard. She could see Drew's house across the pond. She shuddered and went inside.

The writers meeting the following evening was held at the local history museum. Amelia was surprised to see Felicity there. She sat down beside the psychic, who was again dressed in an embroidered kaftan.

Felicity smiled at her and asked, "How's The Magician?"

"I haven't 'seen' him in a while, thank goodness. My visions have been free of the VP."

Felicity stared into Amelia's eyes. "Do you have a direct connection to him now?"

Amelia was stunned by Felicity's question and averted her eyes. "I... um, I can't talk about it."

The meeting began with introductions of the speakers, then a request for everyone present to state their name and why they were in attendance. Most people hadn't published yet, but were working on a variety of projects, from short stories to novels to screenplays. Amelia talked about her desire to write about recent personal events and fictionalize them.

A gentleman seated behind her said he was a journalist but aspired to write novels. He wanted to start a subgroup for new writers. After the meeting, Amelia approached the man and told him she was interested in joining his group.

"That's great," said Gerald Bolton. "We can be a support for each other. Here, put down your name and email, and I'll be in touch."

Four other people wrote down their information for the newly formed "Rookies" group. Amelia was looking forward to getting feedback on her prose. Felicity followed her to the elevator; her psychic antenna was up.

"Seriously, Amelia. I feel something's happened since I last saw you. I'm worried you're in danger."

Amelia stared at her. "I'm not in any danger that I know of. You're right that there's been a direct connection with The Magician, but the authorities are handling it."

"Be careful who you trust," Felicity said as they exited the elevator. "I feel there are several factions that could pose danger. In my mind I'm hearing Gregorian chanting, and getting the fragrance of incense. This could mean a religious connection."

"Thanks for the warning, Felicity. I'll be careful."

Amelia drove home with renewed feelings of anxiety. She hadn't heard any more from the FBI about The Deacons. For the second day in a row, her stomach was in knots and her fear level was high. *I'm in my own personal code orange. Oh no! I have to come up with a new code system. The color orange makes me feel even worse. I can't even eat oranges anymore, and I live in Florida!*

CHAPTER 35

The Farmhouse

*O*nly light and love can dispel the dark.

Amelia typed these words into her computer. She wasn't certain where they came from, yet they seemed important. She wanted to record the confession of Connor Stewart, but before she could put Abby's story into words, she needed to write about her own.

For decades, she'd courageously and quietly dealt with her abduction at age 25. A mentally ill man who grabbed her as she strolled down a quiet city street had randomly chosen her. Michael was away at a business meeting, and she'd been running errands after work. As dusk approached, she was casually walking back to their apartment with a bag of groceries. A van pulled up beside her and the passenger window rolled down. A young man called out to her, asking for directions to a street she'd never heard of.

She quickened her pace. The van remained stationary. Suddenly the vehicle sped up and bounced over the curb, blocking the sidewalk. The well-built man hopped out, grabbed her, and threw her into the back of the van. He slammed the doors shut, jumped into the driver's seat, and drove away. Amelia's groceries lay scattered in the street.

Panicked, she screamed and searched for a way out of the windowless van. The interior door handles had been removed, and the front seat was boarded off from the rear compartment. Amelia shouted for help until her voice was reduced to a whisper. The owner had soundproofed the vehicle. After what seemed like hours, they stopped.

When the van doors finally opened, Amelia saw they were parked beside a darkened farmhouse with a single porch light casting an eerie glow. A small barn was over to the left, and a spotlight shone at the corner of the building. Fields of corn were waving in the night breeze off to the right. Her assailant grabbed her and tied her wrists with a rope. He dragged her kicking and screaming into the barn. He roughly threw her inside, tied her ankles together, and then locked the barn doors from the outside.

The abductor called out through the crack in the door, "I'll be back for you later. Then we'll have a little fun." Amelia surveyed her surroundings, looking for an escape route. Using her teeth, she slowly untied the rope that bound her wrists and undid the rope around her feet. She silently repeated the mantra, *Michael, I'm coming home.*

The barn was almost empty, as if no one had used it for a long time. A dim light came in through several holes in the siding. There was a loft with a small, vented window, but no ladder to access the area. Pale moonlight came in through the window. Amelia took deep breaths to control her panic. There had to be a way out. Suddenly a wave of energy rushed up her spine. From somewhere deep inside welled an intense feeling of courage.

Then she noticed a large hook on a chain that was dangling from the ceiling near a corner of the barn. It was almost within her reach. She found an old chair and placed it underneath the chain. She jumped several times before catching the metal hook.

Using all her strength and her gymnastics training from high school, she pushed off against the side wall of the barn. Over and over she shoved her feet against the wall and swung closer to the loft. Finally, with a mighty push, her legs were able to grasp a wooden post in the loft. Wrapping her legs around the post, she let go of the hook and pulled herself up. Hastily, she grabbed a board and smashed the wooden vent slats covering the window.

Amelia hoisted herself up and through the window. Looking down, she was thrilled to see bales of hay directly below her. She maneuvered her body so that she could jump feet first, and prayed the straw would break her fall. Her prayer was answered as she landed with a thump on the stack of hay and rolled to the ground. Without hesitating, she bolted toward the fields of corn. She ran as fast as she could, zigzagging in and out of the tall rows. She heard her kidnapper screaming in the distance, and saw a flashlight weaving through the corn stalks.

After several minutes, she followed a voice in her head and made a sharp left turn through the field. Almost immediately, she stumbled upon a two-lane highway. She heard her pursuer closing in, but she was able to flag down a car before he caught up to her.

Amelia knew that it could have been much worse. Her abductor, Gavin Glaser, was arrested on the basis of her report to the police. The remains of two women were found behind the barn. He'd inherited the farm from his parents, but lived in the city. The fields were rented out to neighboring farmers, which was why the barn was practically empty.

Glaser had been investigated in his youth for cruelty to animals, but no charges were ever filed. He'd worked as a plumber recently, but had been fired the week before he grabbed Amelia. His firing had been the trigger for his insatiable need to be in control and prove his dominance. In his twisted mind, he felt relief after both of his previous abductions and murders. He had a specific ritual before he assaulted the women. Fortunately for Amelia, that gave her just enough time to escape.

Amelia typed in the final words of her living nightmare into her computer. It popped into her mind that Linda said she'd been with her on her darkest day. Was Linda the one who whispered in her ear to turn left at the perfect moment?

CHAPTER 36

VP

S ecret Service agents accompanied the vice president to his home district in Indiana. Throngs of protesters greeted him at his house. There were also a few supporters waiving Confederate flags and screaming profanities at the critics of the administration.

The VP had tried to maintain a low profile since he'd hired a personal lawyer to defend him on the Russian investigation. As head of the presidential transition team, he was informed multiple times that the disgraced National Security Advisor had lied on numerous occasions about his ties to foreign governments, including Russia and Turkey. Then the VP lied to the country again and again. His 'poor me, I didn't know' act didn't cut it with wide swaths of Americans. And it was obvious the Department of Justice wasn't fooled either. There could be knowledge of illegal activity charges.

The FBI had informed the vice president of the assassination conspiracy. Alton Fry's contact in Washington, Carter Downing, had disappeared. They'd traced his movements until the day that Fry was interrogated. Then nothing. Downing worked for a private security company after retiring from the Secret Service. It was well known that he was a staunch supporter of traditional Catholicism, and it was not surprising to any of his former coworkers that he was involved with The Deacons.

The Bureau investigated every Secret Service agent assigned to the VP, but could not identify any suspects. The detail was summarily dismissed and a new one brought in, just in case. The VP continued to look over his shoulder every time he was in public.

CHAPTER 37

Sister

H ey, Mom. How you doing?" asked Sasha, answering Amelia's phone call.

"Good, Sasha. What have you been up to?"

"I just got home from a book signing at the independent book store down the street. The author looked so much like you I thought you had a long-lost sister."

Amelia laughed. "I don't think there are any additional siblings out there, just the one brother and one sister. What's her name?"

Sasha turned on his computer and sent his mother an email. "Her name's Rose Windsor, and her latest nonfiction book is *The New Politics: A Southern Feminist's View*. I know you'd like it. It's as good as Timothy Snyder's *On Tyranny* and Naomi Klein's, *No Is Not Enough: Resisting T's Shock Politics and Winning the World We Need*. I sent you a link."

Turning on her computer, Amelia opened the email link and was shocked to see a photo of the author. "Oh my gosh, Honey! She does look a lot like me. Even more than my own sister."

"Did you click on her book tour schedule? She's leaving Philly tomorrow and will be at The Book Loft in Fernandina in a couple of days," Sasha said.

"What would I do without you keeping me plugged in to what's going on in the world! Even in my own little town!"

"Mom, I'm glad you're helping the cops and the FBI, but I'm worried about you. There are a lot of crazies out there. Have any more people contacted you about helping them?"

"No, I've stayed off social media and since I got a new my cell number, I've been fine. I promise I'll be careful." Amelia changed the subject. "I've started writing short stories, and I joined a writing group for rookies. Our first meeting is on Thursday at the library."

"That's great. Will you include your unexpected psychic abilities?"

"Yes, at least in one story. I had an interesting encounter with a repairman yesterday. Our washing machine wasn't working properly. The service guy came out and said we had to replace the motor. When I asked him to tell the truth, he admitted it was only a minor part that needed replacing."

"That's wild! I guess there's an upside to this gift," said Sasha. "What else are you going to write about?"

"I want to include a story about my abduction. I'm finally ready to talk about."

"I'm proud of you, Mom. Let me know if I can help. Gotta go. Love you."

"Love you, too."

Amelia stared at the photo of Rose Windsor. She scrolled down to the author's biography. Born and raised in Greenville, SC, Rose attended North Greenville University, a Baptist college affiliated with Freedom University in Virginia. She received her master's degree, specializing in Modern European History, from the University of Cambridge in England. She returned to Cambridge for her PHD in 2001 with a Gates Scholarship from the Bill and Melinda Gates Foundation.

Ms. Windsor had traveled extensively through Western and Eastern Europe. She'd lived in Russia for a year and Germany for several years, where she met her husband, Johann Humbert, who recently transferred to the BMW auto facility in Spartanburg, SC. They resided in Greenville, SC. Rose had returned to her Southern home. There was no mention of any children.

Amelia decided to download Rose's book onto her Kindle and attend the book signing, where she'd pick up a paper copy of *The New Politics*.

It's interesting that Rose studied modern European history and fascism, communism, and totalitarianism like I did. And she definitely could be my younger, prettier sister, Amelia thought.

She opened her notebook to the page where she'd recorded some of the points that author Naomi Klein had made about the present state of affairs. Amelia read some of the things that most impacted her about shock politics.

"The brutal tactic of systematically using the public's disorientation following a collective shock—wars, coups, terrorist attacks, market crashes or natural disasters—to push through radical corporate measures, often called shock therapy... The goal is all out war on the public sphere and the public interest, whether in the form of anti-pollution regulations or programs for the hungry. In their place will be unfettered power and freedom for corporations."

She read about the "naked corporate takeover" and "the deconstruction of the administration state... a full-bore attack on the welfare state and social services... The presidency is in fact the crowning extension of the T brand." Amelia felt sick to her stomach when she thought about the hideous arrogance of 45 and his shameful attacks on women and anyone who stood up to him. The constant lies—now documented at over 1000—and his stupidity made her want to cry. *Hopefully, the country's story will have a positive outcome if enough people stand together against the corporate coup d'état,* she thought. *As long as T doesn't start WWIII, which is a real possibility.*

Amelia was looking forward to Rose Windsor's Southern perspective on the fallout from the election and the direction of the country. The cult-like nature of 45's base was most evident in the South and Midwest. She wanted to ask Rose what it would take to reach the Independents and moderate Republicans in the South. She desperately wanted to build a bridge to those who may listen. She aspired to connect through her writing.

CHAPTER 38

Book Signing

A small crowd congregated outside The Book Loft on Centre Street in Fernandina Beach. Amelia climbed the stairs beside the exposed red brick wall, and greeted several people she'd met at the Women's March and subsequent meetings. The upstairs room was packed; it was standing room only for the author's presentation. Rose Windsor followed Susan, the store's owner, up the stairway and they took their place behind a lectern.

Amelia found a spot to call her own, beside the window that overlooked a massive oak outside. Ms. Windsor was introduced and began her presentation. After several minutes, Rose noticed Amelia and caught her breath.

Amelia smiled at her. *She recognizes how much we look alike. I hope I didn't upset her.* Rose recovered her composure and continued her speech. Her voice was strong, with a distinct South Carolina accent. She was professional, confident, and persuasive in her arguments. She insisted the future of the country was in the hands of ordinary citizens. The grassroots actions were the only way to stop the destruction of democracy in America.

Rose discussed the history of women in the United States, and particularly in the South. Many attendees nodded in agreement when she spoke of the pressure to uphold the 'values' of the religious right, and the traditions of female silence and submission. The 'steel magnolias,' as Southern women are called, were flowers often trapped in a misogynistic, predatory, patriarchal system. The status quo was sustained by both sexes, and the movement toward true equality was still in the future.

She talked briefly about the history of fascism and totalitarianism and pointed out how the new administration had embraced a fascist agenda. The oligarchy in control of the White House threatened to demolish the social progress made during the latter half of the twentieth century. The attacks on the free press, the violence against 'others,' the destruction of public education, and denial of basic healthcare for all citizens concerned the author.

During the Q & A, several people wanted Rose's views on the Russian president's frightening control over 45. The topics of treason through collusion, the emoluments clause violations, and the mental instability of a seemingly senile 71-year-old despot were all covered in detail. Donald Junior's admission that he, his brother-in-law, and the campaign manager met with a Russian lawyer and other Russians tied to the Kremlin to obtain stolen information on Clinton was certainly a step toward a case of collusion. Many felt the Russian dictator was blackmailing the T family because of financial entanglements. Two older men got up and noisily descended the stairs. It was obvious they were not interested in the direction of the conversation.

When Rose had finished her presentation, she signed books for over an hour. She warmly greeted each person—even the elderly gentleman who had interrupted her twice and scowled at her the entire evening. She smiled at the curmudgeon because at least he was buying a book, and may open his heart and mind at some point. Amelia was the last one in line and Rose grinned at her.

"Are we related somehow?" said Rose with a chuckle. "I've never met someone who looks like a sister."

"I was born in Canada. Do you have any relatives in Ontario?" Amelia asked.

"None that I know of. I'm all done for the evening. Are you free to get a cup of coffee or a glass of wine? Maybe we can figure out if we're family."

"That sounds great. I'm Amelia Jones. I'll text my husband and tell him I'll be late. Oh, I love the scarf you're wearing in the author photo on the back cover."

"Thanks, it's an Hermès I got from an old friend of mine. He promised me one when I finished writing the book."

Rose signed Amelia's book, gathered her things, and thanked Susan. She and Amelia strolled down Centre Street to the restaurant at the harbor and ordered a drink at the bar.

"Why did you come to the island for a book signing?" Amelia asked. "It's such a small town."

"I used to vacation here as a child. I always loved Amelia Island, and I'd met Susan several times. When she asked me to come, I jumped at the chance. I'm staying for a few days before I head to Miami for a signing. This tour has been exhausting, but it's really worthwhile. I've met so many great people along the way. Present company included. I'm assuming you've researched me online. Tell me a little about yourself."

Amelia gave Rose a condensed version of her life. They could not find a familial connection, but agreed they looked like sisters. Understanding it was public knowledge, Amelia then revealed the details of her coma and psychic abilities. She briefly described her interactions with the Jacksonville police and the FBI.

"Oh my gosh! You have the makings of a great novel. Have you ever thought about writing?" Rose inquired.

Amelia blushed and sipped her wine. "Actually, I have been considering a short story, or perhaps a novel. I've joined the local writer's group, and hope to start soon. You're a true Southerner; so, how do we reach the Independents and moderates in the South and Midwest?"

Rose sighed and swirled the wine in her glass. "I've struggled with that question since the election. Rational arguments don't work with the president's cult-like followers. They think he speaks like them, and therefore he's on their side. They embrace his bluster and war mongering. His anti-establishment, anti-mainstream media, anti-DC rhetoric hits home, and they turn a blind eye to his lack of accomplishments. It's disheartening, and I'm not sure that most of them will ever admit they've made a mistake."

"I agree that buyers' remorse won't happen to thirty-three percent of his supporters. But what about the more open-minded voters? And what role will women play in the future of this country?" Amelia asked.

A loud crash came from the kitchen, and both women jumped. They laughed at their shared startled response. Suddenly, Amelia could see the aura around Rose. There were soft shades of blue and gold, but there were also flashes of red. *I don't think she's angry. I wonder what the red swirls mean.*

"Rose, are you afraid of something? This may sound strange, but I can see your aura—the energy field around your body. There are flares of red in your otherwise peaceful aura."

Rose looked down at her hands. "You're on track. I've received several threats recently—death threats."

"Oh no! Have you contacted the police?"

"Yes, and my publishers have been in touch with the FBI. They're working to identify where the threats originated. I even received an envelope full of white powder in the mail. It was postmarked in Georgia. The powder was baking soda and wasn't dangerous, but it was a warning."

"What is *wrong* with people? The violence has gotten out of control. And its instigators are at the top. I couldn't believe it when 45 posted a video of him body slamming a person with a CNN logo across his head. This truly is a barbaric administration. So many of his campaign rallies were like those staged wrestling matches. It's sick! Sometimes I wonder if I should move back to Canada."

"I'm not sure I would have returned to the US if my husband hadn't been offered the job at the BMW facility in South Carolina. We liked living in Stuttgart and having such diversity within a short driving distance. Italy is one of my favorite places in the world, and we visited every part of the country. I definitely never intended to live in the South again, but sometimes life has a way of making you face your demons."

Amelia nodded. "Life has given me new demons to face. Or they're really more like paranormal challenges. Visions, seeing auras and bringing out the honesty in people are totally unexpected abilities."

CHAPTER 39

Conspirators

F ather Rathbone entered the public library in Jacksonville. He was dressed in civilian clothes and had a fake library card to access the computers without revealing his identity. He'd been researching ways to end a person's life without anyone suspecting it was murder. The members of the KNC would implement their plan on the three targets when the time was right. Each day brought the likelihood of 45's removal from office closer. They had to stop the Republicans from losing ground in 2018 and 2020.

Rathbone was also motivated by the uncertainty created by his nemesis, the liberal pope in the Vatican. In a short time, four conservative cardinals were out of power. One cardinal died in his sleep, and the Australian was called home to face sexual abuse charges. The head of the Congregation for the Doctrine of the Faith did not have his term renewed, and the final cardinal retired. There was conflict over progressive concepts, including sacraments for remarried people, married priests, same-sex relationships, female deacons, and birth control.

The father's mistress, Sophia, had a brilliant but troubled younger brother, Robert, who was a computer genius. Rathbone had read online about instances of a car's computer being hijacked. There was evidence that a California journalist's car was taken over in June 2013, resulting in a full-speed crash into a tree followed by a fatal explosion. The car's engine had flown through the air over 50 feet. This was just the type of event that could rid them of one of their targets without revealing the origins of the scheme. Robert was capable of hacking a car's computer and making this happen without being traced. The governor would be the target of this attack.

Reverend Miller had contacted an unethical friend with the St. Louis police department and arranged to get a drug that would poison another victim. There were plenty of confiscated drugs, such as the synthetic opioid fentanyl, in evidence lockup. For a price, the drug could be obtained in several forms: powder, pills, or patches, as well as injections. And if that didn't work out, Miller would find someone to order the drug directly from China. The effect of a powerful narcotic on the Marine could be fatal. Details were still being investigated on how to best administer the drug to the victim. This would involve the direct action of Miller.

Dr. Gabriel had devised his own means of eliminating a Democratic contender for 2020. The State Attorney General would meet her untimely demise in a more traditional way. The doctor had a childhood friend who had worked in black ops for the CIA. After retiring, this friend had killed an ex-girlfriend in a jealous rage. Dr. Gabriel provided the man with an alibi. The friend was never charged, and he owed Edgar a very large favor.

A sniper's bullet to the forehead, when she returned to her home in California, was the simple plan. The KNC were moving forward with their deadly scheme. Regardless of what happened with the president and his collusion and incompetence, the accomplishments of the right would be safeguarded.

The members had hoped not to include others in their plot, but this proved to be impossible. Also, Rathbone and Gabriel would protect themselves by not being physically involved in the assassinations. Miller was a gambler by nature and enjoyed the prospect of getting away with murder. The conspirators continued to communicate on burner phones, but used them as little as possible. Millions had been murdered in the name of God, and a few more liberals would soon be added to the list.

CHAPTER 40

French Martinis

Amelia and Rose met for dinner the following evening at Luca's Bistro in downtown Fernandina Beach. There'd been an instant kinship between the women, and both could see a friendship in the future. Over French martinis, they continued their discussion from the night before. They examined how the country had changed since the seismic shock of 9/11, and the continued fear mongering by those presently in power. Rose had left the US for Europe a month before the attack on the World Trade Center, but was affected by it as much as any American citizen.

The blitzkrieg approach of the GOP's attacks on American society was scrutinized. The questions were: Would this multi-pronged trauma overwhelm and exhaust individuals, or help unite them? Could the 4.2 million people who marched on January 21, 2017 continue to make their voices heard and bring back a compassionate republic? Would women be a seismic force of change?

"One thing I hadn't anticipated was the vital role of lawyers as the defenders of democracy," Rose stated. "Right from the start and the first Muslim ban, all types of lawyers—both paid and unpaid—have made incredible contributions to the defense of the Constitution. The Democratic state attorney generals have been amazing, too."

Amelia added, "And the special prosecutor has gathered some of the best legal minds to investigate the Russian connection. There are sixteen top lawyers working for him full time. I expect there's money at the root

of everything. Money laundering, the Russian mafia, and other illegal and immoral dealings are behind 45's unnatural defense of Putin."

"You could be right. I wonder how long it's going to take for a full report to come out. And then what?"

Amelia ordered another round and mulled over Rose's question. "What's happening behind the scenes with the special prosecutor? Will the GOP actually force the tyrant out of office? Will he resign, like Nixon? Or stand up against impeachment proceedings? What about other conspiracies? Will the GOP be able to stop the investigation? And then what would happen?"

Rose laughed. "This is what you should be writing about. Your mind is completely wrapped around this political situation, like cloth around a mummy."

The bartender brought their drinks. "I've never in my life been so affected by anything before. I was completely involved in raising my kids, and I don't regret a minute of it. Maybe I need a cause, now that I'm in the stage between being a full-time mother and a grandmother. Beyond the role of volunteer, I need a passion."

"I think you've found it, Amelia. Your psychic ability notwithstanding, you can take a role in the resistance/persistence movement. And you have the added benefit of making people speak the truth."

The server dropped off menus on their table, and the women decided to continue the conversation over Caesar salad and four-cheese gnocchi. After ordering, Amelia laughed and shook her head.

"What is it?" asked Rose.

"I've been determined to end my harmful white diet. Since the election, my blood pressure and blood sugars are up."

"I haven't heard of a white diet."

"It's my consumption of white bread, white pasta, vanilla ice cream and white wine that's hurting my body. I have to change my ways, because I don't want to go on any more medications. My doctor has given me six months to improve my numbers."

"So French martinis and gnocchi aren't on the list?"

Amelia chuckled. "Absolutely not! Tomorrow I'll get back to my whole grains, low fat, and low sugar diet. And I'll start exercising more."

"I've heard of the T-ten, the extra weight people are putting on after the election. You're not the only one using comfort food to deal with 45."

The server placed the salads and pasta dishes in front of the women and they both giggled. They enjoyed every bite of the food, especially Amelia.

"I grew up in Toronto, then moved to Boston. This is the first time I've lived in the South. What was it like, being raised in South Carolina?" Amelia asked.

"It's funny, but I never felt at home in my family or in the South. I know I wasn't adopted, but the social customs and church dogma seemed foreign to me. There are a lot of wonderful things about the friendship and support Southerners provide to one another, though. There are great traditions and the humor is unsurpassed."

"I love all the creative Southern sayings. They're like a quick wit delivered at a leisurely pace. Truly unique."

"You're right about that. I felt I was unique, and was emotionally distant from my family. To try and fit in, I went to the Baptist-affiliated college that my parents attended. It didn't work. I was always an outsider."

"Is that why you moved away?"

"Yes. I thought that getting out of South Carolina would improve things, and I worked at Freedom University in Virginia for two summers. My dad pulled some strings to get me internships there. The culture was still too conservative, but I met a few people who supported my feminist beliefs. One of my best friends, Bruce Nelson, was a closet gay and a good guy. He was always moody, but now I believe he's bipolar. He's the one who gave me the scarf I wore in the book photo."

"But why did you choose England and not New England for your post-grad degrees?"

"While going through brochures at the college guidance office, I saw photos of the University of Cambridge. It was like an electric shock went through my body. I *remembered* being there. I know that sounds crazy."

Amelia looked up from her salad. "Rose, I believe in past lives, so that's not crazy at all. A part of your soul was there at another time. The memory was embedded in your spirit, and you had a visceral reaction that led to a physical action. That's very cool."

"My family thought I was insane, and a turncoat. Our relationship is still strained, especially since my book was published. They don't appreciate their dirty laundry being exposed. My mother defends the Southern social structure and the Baptist teachings. In the book I talk about the sexual harassment by powerful men that was accepted as 'boys being boys,' and how we were expected to remain silent. She barely tolerates me these days."

"That's so sad. My family isn't happy with my stand on the Catholic Church, but they still support me. My mom even watched the Netflix documentary *The Keepers*, about the nun in Baltimore who was murdered in 1969."

"I haven't heard of that one."

"It's about Sister Cathy Cesnik. She was a teacher at a Catholic girls' high school who discovered that priests were raping students right on the premises. Decades later, a woman uncovered suppressed memories of being attacked and a newspaper article was written about her accounts. This led to others coming forward, and an intense investigation by two former students."

"Were they abused too?" asked Rose.

"No, these two tenacious sixty-something women investigated on their own. They forced the Church to finally acknowledge the criminal actions of the priests and their police officer buddies. The coverup was pure evil, as bad as the murder of Sister Cesnik. Here was a case of sexual assault on young girls that led to homicide."

Rose's phone rang and Amelia told her to answer. Rose left the table and walked outside to take the call. She was smiling when she returned to her dinner.

"You look pleased. What's up?" asked Amelia.

"That was my publicist. I've been invited to speak at a women's forum in DC in a few weeks. Another popular 'feminist' had to pull out and I've been asked to fill in. I certainly don't mind being a replacement speaker."

"How exciting! And it will help you sell your books."

"You're right about that. Most people don't know how hard it is to make a living from being a writer. The author only gets five to seven percent of trade paperback sales. It takes a lot of sales to pay the mortgage. I'm fortunate that my husband is financially successful. It gives me the freedom to write at my own pace."

"Wow, I had no idea that authors were paid so little. I guess I won't be making a fortune from my short stories or a novel."

"You never know, Amelia. With your experiences and psychic abilities, you may just write a best seller!"

CHAPTER 41

Tears of Regret

The morning sped by as Amelia wrote preliminary notes for a novel. She didn't have a complete outline, but ideas were swirling in her head and she wanted to write them down before they disappeared into the ether. In the back of her notebook she penned her thoughts about 45 after his disgusting defense of the KKK, Nazis, and white supremacists at the rally in Charlottesville, Virginia.

She wrote, *He's a grotesque facsimile of a president. He's a Frankenstein's monster, cobbled together by the alt-right—a living, breathing brute without a soul. He's a psychopath with a dark heart, a heart as black as the coal those miners hack out of the deep tunnels. No conscience or compassion. The 900 hate groups active in the US that support him unquestionably need to dissolve.*

When will the Republicans stand up to this fool? When will they put their country before party? Why is it that all the members of the economic, manufacturing, and business advisory councils quit, but the evangelical advisors still support him—except for the single religious leader with a shred of human dignity? Then there's the false equivalency of the white supremacist protestors' actions with those in opposition. Home-grown Nazis are domestic terrorists.

It's obvious that the radical right has been rebranded. They no longer wear hoods, but white golf shirts and beige khakis like their supreme leader. They fundraise on the internet so they don't worry about covering their faces. The KKK should be declared a terrorist organization, and prosecuted as such in every state.

When her sadness became overwhelming, she decided to take a walk around the neighborhood. As she passed Hailey's house, she paused when she saw her neighbor. Amelia walked into the open garage and approached Hailey, who was sitting on a beach chair with her tears pooling in her eyes.

"Hailey! What's wrong? Did something happen to the girls?"

"No, no, they're fine. She was my age! Heather Heyer was my age. That fascist murdered her in Charlottesville. She shouldn't have died for standing up against hatred."

Amelia pulled up chair, sat beside the sorrowful woman and held her hand.

"I can't forgive myself for voting for T. I just wanted a change in Washington," Hailey began. "Someone who'd shake up the establishment and end the gridlock. As a successful businessman, I thought he could bring both sides together. The great negotiator. What a crock! He's gotten nothing done!"

"Many people thought the way you did, Hailey. But too many of them don't regret their decision and continue to support the tyrant," said Amelia. "Including so many in the GOP and his administration. They're cowards of the worst kind when they don't condemn the man by name."

"I chose to ignore what a disgusting, vulgar, sexist pig he is. I justified my vote by chirping 'Benghazi' and 'email scandal' like a demented puppet. How naïve I was, buying into the cult of celebrity. I'm ashamed to admit I believed in him. I literally feel sick to my stomach."

The women were silent for a long time as Hailey pulled a tissue from her pocket and dried her tears of regret.

"So, how can we honor Heather's life and death like her mother spoke about at the funeral service? What action can we each take to rid this country of the troll in the Oval Office and send him back to his golden New York palace? Or even better, a prison cell for money laundering. I can't believe he called the White House a dump."

Hailey sighed. "I wish I lived in a dump that nice. James and I both hoped he'd become presidential and rise to the occasion when he was in office. Boy, were we wrong! When he speaks from his heart it's obvious that he supports the neo-Nazis and white supremacists. He parrots Fox news and Breitbart and their evil rhetoric. What the hell is the alt-left?"

"He's done more to perpetuate fake news than anyone alive. We need to do more than complain. Actions speak louder than words." Amelia got to her feet and hugged her neighbor. "Let me know if you have any scathingly brilliant ideas about how we can make a positive change. See you later."

"Thanks, I will."

Amelia continued her stroll around the neighborhood. Some days she wished all that had happened since the election wasn't real, that it was all just a bad dream. Her pace was slow and her heart was heavy. A black cloud swept across the sun and thunder rolled in the distance. She started to jog home before the impending storm reached her.

As she dashed into the house, a wave of emotion enveloped her. She dropped into an armchair and let the feelings wash over her. *I'm going to have an impact on the national stage, but the public won't know about it.* She had no idea where the thought came from. She turned on her computer and opened a new Word document. Then a stream of ideas flowed through her fingers as she typed for 20 minutes. When she was finished, she was shocked by the words on the page. *It's like I was channeling information! What's next on this crazy ride?*

CHAPTER 42

St. Mary's River

Two boys trudged down the woodland path toward the river. Paul and Rich were hauling fishing poles, camping gear, and backpacks filled with food and bait. They found the perfect spot for their overnight stay, and quickly set up camp. After anchoring the tent and securing their food inside, they picked up the fishing rods and made their way to the river.

St. Mary's River in the Maryland state park was the boy's favorite place for their fishing expeditions. They chattered about their dreams to camp in all the national parks in America. They couldn't wait to grow up and find some real adventure. The state park was as far as their parents would allow the thirteen-year-old boys to go. When they got their drivers licenses, they'd plan the gradual fulfillment of their vision.

They made their way along the shoreline to an outcropping of boulders. Casting their lines into the flowing water they settled in for afternoon, hoping to hook a big one. Within minutes, there was a tug on one of the lines. Paul yelled for help as he began reeling in the line, struggling with the weight of his fish.

Rich held the rod as Paul reeled in the catch, but he screamed and dropped the pole when he saw a body hooked on his line. It was a man in a dark suit, floating face down. The hook had snagged the back of the jacket. Rich rushed down and pulled the body onto the shore. Carefully he turned the corpse over as Paul cautiously approached. A blackened face with vacant eyes stared up at them. There was a distinct hole in the middle of the man's forehead.

Paul let out a blood-curdling scream. Rich took out his cell phone and tried to get service. He ran up the hill toward their camp, finally got reception, and called 911. He rushed back to Paul and tried to comfort his hysterical friend.

The ex-Secret Serviceman and conspirator with The Deacons, Carter Downing, had finally reappeared.

CHAPTER 43

Writer's Group

A melia was excited to meet with the newbie writers in the Rookies group. She was a little late, and the meeting was just getting underway when she arrived. Gerald was asking the attendees to tell the others about who they were and what they hoped to accomplish. The first two elderly women had decided to write memoirs so their life stories weren't lost with their passing. The tales their parents and grandparents told to them should be recorded before their memories failed from addled minds.

A long-winded older gentleman gave a full account of his life story and his desire to write historical fiction. Gerald finally cut him off. A young woman wanted to write children's books inspired by the antics of her three small boys. When it was Amelia's turn, she briefly described her life, the accident, her coma, and the special gift she now possessed.

"I recognize you," the young woman began. "I saw you on YouTube."

Amelia blushed. This was the opening Gerald had been waiting for. Unbeknownst to the group, he was a reporter for the gossip magazine *Did You Hear?* and its internet counterpart. He and his photographer, Drew had pitched the story of the woman who had demonstrated she could make people speak the truth. It was a unique ability, even in the crazy world of gossip publications.

Gerald had purposely gone to the Writers by the Sea meeting in the hope of meeting Amelia and getting her story. The ruse had worked, and he gently pressed her on details of her experiences. She confided more than she normally would, feeling safe with a local group of like-minded people. She even spoke of working with the Fernandina Beach police, Jacksonville police, and the FBI.

"I bet you can't make me tell the truth," grumbled the older man. "Go ahead, try it."

Amelia glared at the man while the others encouraged her to try. She hesitated then the old man laughed and mocked her again.

"You're a fraud. It's bullshit," he said.

"You really think so? I'm not sure how it works or even if it will, but here goes. Have you ever stolen anything? The truth be told."

The man shuddered, coughed, and mumbled, "No, I'm not a thief." He continued to squirm in his chair. "Only, only that one time I embezzled money from my employer. I—I needed the money. I paid them back, I *swear* I paid them back!"

The room was quiet as the man picked up his briefcase and stormed out. Gerald had recorded the exchange on his phone, and couldn't wait to submit the story. He now had direct evidence of Amelia's capabilities that would back up the other examples Drew had collected, including video from the hospital and Marvin Darby's confession.

"I think that's all for tonight," Gerald said.

Everyone gathered their belongings and headed for the door.

"That's a powerful and scary gift you have, Amelia," stated the young woman. "I wouldn't be comfortable with that ability."

Amelia drove home with the radio blaring. She wanted to drown out the critic in her head who was lambasting her for revealing so much to a group of strangers. She was confident that none of the people would broadcast what had happened that night, but she couldn't be sure. *Why, oh why did I just do that? I didn't want to, but that geezer made me so angry. I'll have to develop a thicker skin if I'm going to survive this new talent.*

CHAPTER 44

Harvey

Amelia turned on the TV after sleeping in late the next morning, and was overwhelmed by more bad news. Hurricane Harvey had pummeled Texas. The 500-year storm and 51 inches of rainfall had devastated the area. She'd purposely not watched the news for several days, and wasn't aware how horrible the storm had been and how desperate the situation had become.

"But global warming is a Chinese hoax! Climate change isn't real," she yelled sarcastically at the television. Michael rushed out of the office.

"Honey, what's wrong?"

Amelia dropped into a chair and covered her face with her hands. Slowly, she looked at her husband.

"One catastrophe after another. Political and natural disasters are assaulting this country. How much more can we take?"

"I don't know. I've been following the reports online. Whole parts of Houston and surrounding areas are underwater. Evacuations have proceeded effectively. The country learned a lot after Hurricane Katrina. The response teams are well coordinated this time."

"Those poor people. So many have lost everything. I can't imagine how long it will take to get things back to normal. We'll have to contribute to the recovery effort."

"The scientists have been saying for years that climate change won't impact how many hurricanes there are, but the intensity will increase.

Even a one or two degree rise in the temperature of the ocean can make a huge difference," said Michael. "Each Celsius degree higher can hold up to seven percent more water. The more water in the hurricane winds, the stronger they can become."

"I hope Hurricane Matthew last year is the only major storm this area will see as long as we're alive," answered Amelia.

"Don't count on it, Honey. Global warming is an 'Inconvenient Truth,' as Al Gore said. This may only be the start of more catastrophes."

Michael went back to the office and left his wife wondering what would happen next. She turned off the news and pondered what she had written in her channeling session. She had no idea what some of it meant, but it was clear to her that there were serious conspiracies by fringe groups swirling around the country. And surprisingly, they involved religious groups. The trillium, a wildflower found in the forests she and her childhood friends frequented, kept popping into her mind.

The doorbell rang, making her jump. Amelia opened the front door and was relieved to see a smiling Ruby with an arm full of flowers.

"Hello there. My garden is overflowing, and I thought you could use a little beauty in your life."

"Ruby! They're amazing. Please come in. I'll get a vase."

The women went into the kitchen and arranged the flowers. The doorbell rang again, startling the ladies. Amelia went to the front door. Felicity was on the porch with two large candles in her arms.

"Oh my! Felicity, please come in. How did you find me?"

"You gave me your card with your cell number and address. The number was out of service, so I thought I'd take a chance that you were home. I made these candles for you."

"Thanks so much. I forgot I gave you the card. And I had to change my number after I was on YouTube and my cell was included in a post on Facebook."

They joined Ruby in the kitchen, and introductions were made. The women discussed the horror of Hurricane Harvey and the concern that people's denial of the seriousness of the impact of seven billion inhabitants on the earth contributed to the problem.

"Felicity, have you ever done any automatic writing, where you channeled information?" Amelia asked.

"Not for many years. Did you get some insight into The Magician?"

"Who's the magician?" Ruby questioned.

"I've had visions of the VP dressed as a magician, and I pulled that Tarot card the first time I met Felicity. No, it wasn't about him, but a trio of religious figures. I wasn't sure of their denominations, although one was probably a Catholic priest. It felt like they were conspiring, but I couldn't identify their targets. I only knew that it was political."

Felicity closed her eyes and took a few deep breaths. The women waited anxiously for the psychic to break her silence. It was another five minutes before Felicity spoke.

"I've had this malaise for several days now. I feel something evil may happen to several elected officials. I agree with your channeled information that there are religious figures at the root of the plot. I'm going to need more time to get a clearer picture."

The doorbell rang one more time. "I wonder if it's Lyla, intuitively knowing we're having a get-together," Amelia said as she headed to the front hall. She opened the door and was surprised to see a clean-cut young man in a white golf shirt and beige khakis standing on the porch.

"Can I help you?"

The man's eyes narrowed and a sneer crossed his face. "Are you Amelia Jones?"

Amelia started to close the door but he pushed it open and grabbed her by the neck. She fell back against the wall and tried to scream.

"I've been sent by God to rid the world of another witch!" the man hissed in her ear.

With her fisted hands, she thrust her arms between her attacker's arms, pushed outward and for a moment broke his grasp. In that instant she screamed for her husband.

Back in the grip of her assailant, Amelia struggled until Michael ran toward them and grabbed the man around the neck. He pulled the moron back and they crashed into the dining room table. The other women ran into the room and saw Amelia holding her neck and Michael struggling with the intruder. Immediately, Ruby gave the man a swift kick to the groin, and he screamed in pain.

151

As he writhed on the floor, Felicity took off her scarf and tied his hands together with the colorful piece of silk. Michael took out his phone and called the police.

"What the hell?" Amelia cried out. "Why did you do this?"

The young man looked up at her with a sinister but pained grin. "I won't be the last," he muttered. "Satan's servants must be stopped."

CHAPTER 45

Did You Hear?

The Fernandina Beach police station was buzzing with activity. Beauregard Hanover had been taken into custody after the attack and was being processed. Amelia and Michael were seated on a bench waiting for someone to give them information on the assailant.

After what seemed like an hour, Officer Flores invited them into a conference room and asked them to be seated. Coffee and bottled water were offered and declined. The officer opened a laptop and brought up the latest edition of the online form of the gossip magazine *Did You Hear?*

The Joneses stared in shock as photos of Amelia on the lanai at their house, in the downtown coffee shop, and at the hospital were on the front page. The headline read, "The Human Lie Detector." Gerald Bolton wrote the article, illustrated with photos by Drew Cavendish.

"Oh, my God! Gerald is the guy from the writer's group, and Drew is the orderly! This is insane, and a total violation of privacy!" Amelia yelled.

Michael jumped up and began pacing. "There's got to be a way to make them take this off the internet. Amelia's going to be the target of every unstable person in Florida."

"What can we do?" she asked.

"You can ask them to delete the photo of your house, but the others were taken in public places. That's how Mr. Hanover found you—he recognized the unique color of your home. He knew your subdivision from the description in the article."

Amelia pushed down the tears and a new, unexpected wave of emotion washed over her. The energy of a soldier rushed up her spine. It was like she'd been infused with the fortitude of an Amazonian warrior. She had called on this strength once before, and she would embrace it again. She stood up and opened her purse.

"Thank you, Officer Flores. Here's my new cell number, if you have any more information."

Amelia marched out of the room, followed closely by her startled husband. On the drive home they were silent. Once they were inside, Amelia went straight to her computer and sent an email to Gerald and to the online magazine. She demanded that the article be removed from the site, and stated that it should not be included in their paper edition. She typed in the name and phone number of her attorney to let Bolton and the publisher know she meant business.

She read the article in full. It detailed her first experience with the doctor and nurse after her coma; the YouTube video of the developer at the city hall meeting; the video of the Georgia congressman in Savannah; an interview with a local officer about the Marvin Darby confession; a friend of Katrina's talking about the arrest of Connor Stewart and Amelia's role in the story; and finally, the recorded discussion at the Rookies writers' meeting and Gerald's personal account of witnessing her ability.

Michael came into the office and handed her a glass of wine. "Do you want to talk about it?"

"Not right now, Love. I need time to process everything."

Michael kissed her cheek and left her to work out her feelings. She opened a new file and began writing about her latest unprecedented experience. This wasn't the time to break down, and surprisingly she didn't want to. Her cellphone rang, and she answered it quickly.

"Hey, Mom. What's up?"

"Oh, Ben. It's so good to hear your voice. I was just about to email you, Sasha, and Lottie. I...I had an unwelcome visitor. A crazy man came to the house and attacked me."

"Mom! Are you OK?"

"Yes. Your dad stopped him, and Ruby and Felicity helped. Thank goodness, I wasn't here alone. Ruby kicked him between the legs. It was quite a sight. I'm not opening the front door again without knowing who it is."

"Why the hell did he do it?"

"Unfortunately, my fifteen minutes of fame isn't over. There was an article in an online gossip magazine about my ability to make people tell the truth. A man in my writer's group wrote it. He must have purposely created the group to get the story. At the meeting, there was a grumpy old man who goaded me into showing them my gift. It was really dumb on my part to fall for it. And there were photos of me, including one of the back of our house. The orderly from the hospital took the photo. That's how the maniac found me."

"But why did the guy attack you?"

"He said he saw the article and God told him to 'kill the witch.' He was dressed like those white supremacists who marched in Charlottesville."

"Mom, it's not your fault. It's that jerk who wrote the story that's wrong, and the nut who attacked you. Man, what is going on? This country has gone insane."

"We have to keep standing up to the fanatics who have been given the permission to act like criminals. This administration continues to condone violence, and it's shameful."

"What's the name of the magazine? I'm going to contact them and get them to take the article off. At least I'll try."

"Thanks, Honey. I'll send you the link now. Talk to you soon."

Amelia sent the link to the article to her children and her friends. She went into the living room to see if there were any news vans outside, and was grateful the street was empty. She wasn't sure how long it would take for the local news to pick up the story. She called her mother to tell her the short version of the tale. She didn't want her mom to worry about her unusual daughter.

CHAPTER 46

Trillium

Special Agent Gilchrist received the information that Carter Downing's body had been found floating in a Maryland river. He threw a stapler across the room in frustration.

"Another dead-end—literally," he grumbled.

Alton Fry honestly didn't know the names of the Secret Service agents involved with The Deacons and the ongoing threat to the VP. Gilchrist's investigation into the Miami of Ohio alumni had turned up nothing. Downing had been the key to solving the mystery.

He debated whether to call Amelia Jones with the news, but felt he owed it to her for assisting his investigation, one that probably lead to the death of Carter Downing. He had hoped to use Amelia again when Downing surfaced, but that wouldn't happen now.

Special Agent Mannford sauntered over and flopped into the chair beside Gilchrist's desk.

"Guess you heard. Now what?"

Gilchrist got up and retrieved the stapler. He slammed it down on the desk.

"Damn it. I don't know. The DC Bureau checked out every member of the Secret Service detail, especially the Catholics and we've got nothing. I'm going to call Mrs. Jones and give her an update."

"Speaking of Mrs. Jones, did you see the article in that rag mag?" asked Mannford.

"No, what magazine?"

Mannford walked to his desk and picked up a print copy of *Did You Hear?* that he'd bought at the newsstand.

Gilchrist groaned when he saw the photos and skimmed the article. "Jeez, this isn't good. I'll give her call."

When the agent spoke to Amelia, she filled him in on the attack after the online publication was released. She had ongoing fears that more deranged people were lying in wait to harm her. She told him the Fernandina police were patrolling her street on a regular basis, and they'd asked local news teams to stay away from her house. Gilchrist informed her of Downing's demise, and told her that the investigation had gone cold.

"Are you certain that Fry hasn't found out about me?" Amelia questioned. "With that online article, I'm worried The Deacons will target me too."

"I'm absolutely positive no one from this office has released your identity or your part in the interrogation. The only visitors Fry has gotten are his lawyer and his sister. I'm guessing you haven't seen the print edition of the article."

"Oh God. No, I haven't seen it."

"Please be careful."

"I will. By the way, I don't think this is related, but I had some impressions the other day about another conspiracy. I got images of three: a trillium wildflower that has three petals, and the trinity. There were religious connotations, too. I'd don't believe it had anything to do with the VP or The Deacons, but I felt a Catholic connection. Maybe I'm losing my mind!"

"I'm not aware of any other conspiracies at this time. I seriously thought we'd be looking at the left fringe as a threat, but it seems the administration has as many enemies on the far right. This whole political situation is unprecedented."

"I've heard the word *unprecedented* a thousand times since the election. Thanks for the update, Agent Gilchrist. Please let me know if I can do anything else to help."

"Will do."

Amelia turned on the TV to watch the news, and saw the devastation in Texas and Louisiana. Switching to the Weather Channel, she saw the newest projected path of Hurricane Irma. It was headed for Florida, but they weren't certain where it would make landfall. It looked like the Keys could be facing a direct hit, after numerous islands in the Caribbean.

"Holy crap! Michael, have you seen the latest on Irma?"

Amelia rushed into the office and saw her husband watching the hurricane's path on his computer. "What do you think?" he asked.

"I guess Sasha is going to have some company. How's it possible that two hurricanes could strike the island in less than a year? There have only been two close to Fernandina in the past hundred and nineteen years!"

"Climate change, like I keep saying. There's deadly flooding in India, too. They haven't even finished the repairs in the Fernandina harbor from Hurricane Matthew. I'll call Sasha, then put the outdoor furniture in the garage. Thank God we have a roof and windows that will survive a category three hurricane."

"And we're a mile in from the ocean, so I don't imagine we'll get flooding. I'm glad we have flood insurance, just in case."

"I'll get gas. There's bound to be a run on the gas stations," said Michael.

"I'll pack enough clothes for a week. Even if the hurricane doesn't make a direct hit, the power could be out for several days."

They went into high gear preparing for their evacuation. Amelia forgot all about Fry, Hanover, and everything else that had been going on. Escaping the storm was her only priority. She texted Lyla and Ruby to make sure they were leaving too.

CHAPTER 47

Irma

Traffic was heavy but moving steadily on northbound Highway 95. Amelia noticed that every time there was any kind of car on the side of the road, people put on their brakes. No one was speeding, but most drivers were very tense.

"What strange times we live in. Mother Nature is making the general malaise in the country worse. Even the hurricane is erratic; it's going to the west side of Florida, then the east, then back to the west," said Amelia.

"It's like the T administration, flip-flopping and unpredictable," added Michael. "But the Keys will be a direct hit after the US Virgin Islands and other parts of the Caribbean."

"It looks like Puerto Rico will be spared."

Amelia was lost in thought. She was careful not to doze off or go into a light trance. She wasn't up for another vision.

"Do you remember when I told you about my vision of a bomb hitting Japan? Now North Korea has fired two missiles over the country. What I didn't get right was that sirens blared in Japan after the missiles were launched. I saw it on a news report. I guess I'm new at this intuition thing."

The drive to Philadelphia was uneventful, and gas was plentiful at this early stage of the evacuation. The Joneses listened to constant updates on MSNBC on XM radio. Every so often, they'd switch to music, but kept getting drawn back to the hurricane reports. It was addicting, even though it had been less than a year since they listened to the coverage during their

Hurricane Matthew evacuation. The trip took over 14 hours because of heavy traffic in Richmond, Virginia and Washington, DC.

Sasha greeted Michael and Amelia at his apartment in South Philly. "I'm so glad you guys decided to get out now," he said. "And Mom, I can't believe you were attacked in the house!"

Amelia hugged her eldest son. "I'm OK, Sweetie. I'm not going to let a crazy man intimidate me. There's so much breaking news these days I'm sure the story in the gossip magazine will soon be forgotten."

"When the article was posted on Facebook, I go so many texts from high school friends wanting to know how you were. I told everyone that you were tough and resilient."

"Thanks, Love. I do feel a new strength and resolve. I won't let anyone make me cower. The attack gives me more ideas for a novel, and I'm determined to write about it."

They got settled in the spare bedroom while Sasha prepared a late dinner. He'd requested time off work to be with his parents. After dinner, they continued to watch the hurricane devastate Barbuda and other islands. Amelia received a text from Lyla, saying that they were hunkering down and would not evacuate. It looked like Irma was headed to the west part of Florida.

"Lyla is staying on the island. I hope they'll be all right. My concern is that even if there isn't a major impact, the power will be out for several hours or even days. I know Ruby and her family went to stay with relatives in Macon."

Several other texts followed, from Amelia's family in Canada and friends across the country. Rose Windsor sent a message as well, offering her home if they needed refuge from the storm.

"Wow, I just got a text from Rose saying we could stay with her in South Carolina. She doesn't even know me well. That's true Southern hospitality."

"I've thought about moving further south," said Sasha. "My job in finance is going well, but in the long term I want to teach high school. I'm not sure what my next step will be."

"You can always live with us in Fernandina if you want to go back to school," added Michael. "We'd be happy to have you. And it would be great to have another seafood lover in the house. I can't believe we live on an island and your mom doesn't like fish."

"Next life, Honey. I promise," answered Amelia.

"I'll think about it, Dad. I need to investigate the best way of getting a teaching degree. I've done some volunteer work with teens, and I know I could relate to them and really be effective."

"I can definitely see you teaching, Sasha. You've always been a leader and great with kids," said Amelia.

"Thanks, Mom. Oh, did Ben tell you he turned down the job in Toronto? He decided it wasn't the right position for him."

"And I'm sure he doesn't want to move even further north. Maybe we should try and talk him into moving to Florida, too," said Michael.

"Do you think your sister will ever move back to the East Coast?" Amelia asked.

"Not too likely, Mom. She loves the Bay area."

Tours of Philadelphia occupied the next few days and kept them from worrying about the hurricane. Sasha enjoyed showing his parents the city, and they had great family discussions over delicious dinners. Sasha had become a good cook since graduating from college.

Hurricane Irma did move toward the west part of Florida, yet Jacksonville had major storm surges and historic flooding along the St. John's River. Amelia Island was spared the worst of the storm, but power was out for several hours, and even days in some areas. Ancient oak trees lost limbs or uprooted completely, taking down power lines. Leaves were stripped from trees and the salt spray from the ocean devastated other plants. In addition to the hurricane, there were two major earthquakes in Mexico in a very short time. The earth was in chaos in too many places.

When Amelia and Michael returned home, they were grateful their new house was fine except for the satellite dish on the roof that had been dislodged. The beach erosion was extensive. Many residents lost their boardwalks, and the dunes were eroded by more than ten feet in some areas. It was nothing compared to the experiences in the Caribbean and Florida Keys. Yet the climate change deniers were still spewing their nonsense.

CHAPTER 48

Shelter

F ather Rathbone welcomed evacuees from Hurricane Irma into the Jacksonville Catholic Church the first night of the storm. Sophia and Robert were among those seeking shelter, and they were ushered into the priest's office.

"Glad you two agreed to come. No sense in taking a chance in your basement apartment," Rathbone said once the door was closed behind his guests. He was careful not to get too close to Sophia when they were in public. Even Robert didn't know about their physical relationship. Sophia's brother was dependent on her, and was excited about being part of a conspiracy. He didn't care about the end results of his actions, only that he could help Sophia. As a devout Catholic, he trusted the priest was working on God's behalf.

Sophia smiled. "We're grateful you sent Anthony to pick us up. It was difficult going through Hurricane Matthew last year."

"Robert, about that special project you were working on? Do you have the Governor's VIN number? Can you access his car's computer?"

Robert snickered. "No problem, Padre. Ya want me to do it the next time he's in the car?"

"No, no. Not yet. I'll send you a text when it's time. You two should get something to eat. Let's go back to the hall."

The father had avoided going to the Opus Dei office in recent weeks. His intuition told him that the building was under surveillance. He wasn't sure if it was because of the KNC operation or that idiot Fry, who had been caught by the FBI and was sitting in prison.

He was also concerned about the ex-CIA black ops guy in Virginia whom Dr. Gabriel had commissioned to assassinate the State Attorney General. Rathbone's sixth sense was working overtime on that connection. And Josh Miller was a loose cannon who caused Henry Rathbone anxiety in the early morning hours when the priest was supposed to be deep in prayer.

What Father Rathbone didn't know was that Reverend Miller had secured a deadly opioid to eliminate the Marine. He'd been investigating means of administering the drug without being caught. He watched movies and television shows about unsolved murders that included poisoning. Not finding an adequate solution to the problem, he decided to call Edgar Gabriel to ask him to contact his black ops friend for practical advice.

Edgar had accidentally left his burner phone at Bruce's apartment. Bruce heard a ringing phone, and it took him several minutes to locate the device in the nightstand drawer. The caller had hung up by then and sent a text asking the doctor to call Josh. There was an earlier text as well, from someone only identified as 'H.'

Bruce felt a knot in his stomach wondering who was calling his long-time love. Sharing the doctor with his wife was one thing, but another man—or other men—was frightening. He'd invested too much into the relationship, and he was no longer a young man. Bruce didn't want to find out if he'd be able to find love again. He decided to do everything in his power to keep his relationship with Edgar.

Dr. Gabriel had seemed distracted recently. Bruce felt his partner was keeping secrets, and he'd searched Edgar's computer when the doctor was in the shower. Bruce was shocked to see lists of prominent Democrats and their biographies. He was puzzled and couldn't imagine that Edgar would move to the political left. If he was, Bruce was excited to think that if Gabriel came out and admitted their affair, they could openly live together. Then his emotions spiraled downward and he wondered if Edgar was planning on leaving his wife and Bruce for another man.

CHAPTER 49

45 Ways

A fter pandering to poor whites to win the election, he quickly proposed policies that would devastate rural working-class whites, while at the same time stocking his cabinet with a record number of billionaires and Wall Street tycoons," Amelia read out loud. The passage came from the book *The Resistance Handbook: 45 Ways to Fight T*, by Markos Moulitas and Michael Huttner. She closed the paperback and placed it on the coffee table. "And there hasn't been a backlash from his base about the wealthy swamp monsters."

Lyla sipped her iced tea as the women relaxed on the lanai, watching seven young mallard ducks trailing behind their mother on the pond. "I guess that reinforces the idea that the election of 45 was more about cultural issues than financial. It was the anger and fears of white people about their place in American society and the threat of non-white people, especially immigrants."

"You're right," Amelia began. "It amazes me that his supporters don't care about any of the White House scandals, from the obvious Russian attack on the election, to the money that has flowed into his coffers despite the emoluments clause, to the fact that T's daughter, son-in-law, and others used personal email accounts for government business."

"Why don't we hear, 'lock them up' about his kids?" Lyla added. "And he doesn't seem to care about the devastation to Puerto Rico from Hurricane Maria. The destruction has been unimaginable, and 45 talks about how they owe billions of dollars to Wall Street and the banks. He personally left them with a $33,000,000 debt when his golf course in Puerto Rico filed for bankruptcy. He isn't concerned about the fact they have no clean water, electricity, gas, or phone service. And then he boasts that Puerto Ricans are saying he's doing a great job."

"That, Lyla, is a psychopath's lack of empathy. And his personal attacks on the mayor of San Juan are disgusting."

"His verbal assault on the NFL players and owners is a sure sign of a mentally unstable old man throwing red meat to his savage base. But the scariest is the Twitter feud with the crazy leader of North Korea. We need cool heads and diplomacy, not childish insults on Twitter. It makes the dispute personal when T calls the leader 'little rocket man.'"

"The administration needs to give the new United Nations economic sanctions time to work," Amelia added.

Lyla rose and walked to the edge of the pond. "Any more fallout from that gossip magazine article?"

Amelia joined her friend, and they watched a snowy egret and blue heron land beside the ducks in the rippling water. "There's nothing new. The local police are certain Hanover was a lone wolf. I spoke to Drew and told him to never, ever take my photo again. He acknowledged the danger he put me in. And the FBI believes the conspiracy against the VP has been thwarted."

"So you're out of the news and out of danger. That's very good."

"Yes," Amelia replied. "And that's why I've decided to accept Rose's invitation to go to the women's forum in Washington. No matter how much people connect online, it's still important to physically be with others. Here, listen to this."

Amelia picked up the book she'd placed on the table and found the page she was looking for. She read: "'People are more effective when they work together, in person...megachurches are a critical component of conservative political organizing: they provide a physical space for people to establish deep connections and a shared sense of identity.'"

"That makes sense. They're now finding that children learn better from real teachers rather than those on a screen. And the disabled people who protested the latest healthcare bill that would devastate Medicaid and preexisting conditions, were wise to be in the Capital building in person.

It was terrible to watch dozens of people in wheelchairs dragged out and arrested."

"Thank God for John McCain and Susan Collins. They are senators with a conscience and the backbone to stand up for what's right. At least for now. We'll see if they betray their principles when the tax plan is up for a vote. It's bad enough the Republicans are openly sabotaging the Affordable Care Act. And that deplorable Health and Human Services secretary spent over a million dollars on private planes in a few months. Drain the swamp, my *ass*."

Michael opened the screen door and joined the women. "Are you two still talking politics?"

Lyla and Amelia nodded.

"I was just reading a report suggesting the reason behind the push for the healthcare bill was that the Republican's wealthy backers are threatening not to support the GOP if they don't get tax reform done—in their favor, of course. And the healthcare bill is part of it," Michael said.

Michael's phone rang, and Amelia knew it was their daughter when he said, "Hi, little Love," as he always did when Lottie called. After several minutes, Michael handed the phone to his wife. "Your turn." Michael and Lyla walked into the house, continuing the healthcare conversation. Amelia settled into a chair to talk to her daughter.

"Hi, Lottie, how are you?"

"Mum! I just received an invitation to a women's forum in DC. My boss said they'd pay for my flight and hotel."

"Oh my gosh, Honey. That must be the same one that Rose invited me to. Now I'm even more excited to go. I get to see my California daughter. If you do run for Congress someday, you could end up in Washington."

Lottie laughed. "You're way ahead of yourself, Mum. But it will be interesting to be with people at the forefront of the women's movement. I'll email you my travel information. We can meet for dinner the first night."

"And I'll introduce you to Rose. She's a smart, talented writer and activist—one with a distinctly Southern accent. We're staying at the Mayflower Hotel."

"Isn't that where Attorney General Sessions met with Russian Ambassador Kislyak last year, and then couldn't recall the meeting?"

"You're right, Lottie, it is! Maybe there'll be other political intrigue when we're there."

"As long as we're not in any danger, I'm up for a little mystery. I'll book a room at the Mayflower, too."

CHAPTER 50

Social Media

R ose Windsor called her old friend Bruce, and knew at once that he was in the depressed phase of his bipolar disorder. To lighten his spirits, she invited him to the women's forum in Washington, and offered to pay for his hotel room.

"You can meet my new friend from Florida. Amelia Jones has acquired a unique ability since she was in a coma. You may have seen her on YouTube, or in that awful gossip magazine, *Did You Hear?* She can make people tell the truth."

"That's impossible, Rose. You're putting me on."

"Check out the online videos. She's helped the local police and even the FBI with cases. She's the real deal."

"Well, I'll take your word for it. Thanks for inviting me, Rose. Can't wait to see you in person. It's been too long."

"I'll send you the details."

Rose hung up, and had an uneasy feeling about her friend. She knew his battle with the mental disorder had been getting worse over the years. Any major difficulty could throw him into an emotional tailspin. Bipolar people battled depression in the down stage, and erratic behavior in the manic stage. She sent Bruce the women's forum itinerary and a loving note in an email.

Bruce read the note and smiled. In an instant, he decided to prove his loyalty to Gabriel; he would invite the doctor to stay with him at the

DC hotel. They needed time alone together, and this was the perfect opportunity.

Needing to uplift her own mood, Rose called her new friend. Amelia answered on the first ring.

"Hi, Rose. I'm excited about the forum in DC."

"I'm happy you're able to come. I just invited my friend Bruce—the guy who gave me the Hermès scarf. I think the two of you will get along well."

"And my good news is that Lottie will be there, too. You can meet my wonderful daughter. It's like the stars are aligning to make this a great trip."

"You can use some positive energy, after that horrible attack. Are you sure you're OK?" Rose asked.

"I fine, really. It's spurred me to continue writing, and keep resisting the hatefulness this president encourages. I won't let right-wing nuts intimidate me. But I also won't open the front door to strangers."

"I'll make dinner reservations for the first night you're in town. You can invite Lottie, and I'll ask Bruce and Jenna, my publicist, to join us."

"That's what I can strive for—having a publisher and a publicist."

"You know I'll do whatever I can to help, Amelia. I have a great editor, when you finish your manuscript."

"This is a conversation I never imagined having. Then again, I never thought I'd have a near-death experience and return with a paranormal ability. Or that I'd be famous on social media."

"And my, oh, my, have you followed the story on the Russian meddling in the election through the postings on social media?" Rose asked. "Russian propaganda fed to Americans in mediums we created. Absolutely frightening!"

"Facebook, Google and Twitter dropped the ball. Facebook is finally admitting that over a hundred and fifty million people saw ads generated by the Russians. My God, they were even paid in rubles for some of them. And thirty-nine states' elections apparatus were hacked by the Russians. We've got to do something before the midterms in 2018."

"It's persistence in the long term, by each and every one of us, that will force a change. Democrats have to get the party unified before next year. Infighting will only lead to the status quo, and that's not acceptable."

"Rose, who do you think the leaders of the Dems will be, going forward?"

"I actually compiled a list last week. The old guard includes Elizabeth Warren, Joe Biden, and Bernie Sanders. But that's not the route to go. Others include Kamala Harris, Kirsten Gillibrand, Terry McAuliffe, Tim Ryan, and Seth Moulton. I'm not sure who's going to rise to the top."

"I hope it's someone who can defend the traditional ideas of inclusion and social progress, but who can also engage white Middle America. We need to move forward, not backward to the 'good old days' that only existed for some Americans. And I pray we can move from hate-filled division to civility, and even kindness and caring for all citizens."

"Amelia, we also have to work on the local levels to elect Democrats."

"I totally agree. I went to a Dems dinner the other night, and there were seventy-five people there. This part of Florida is traditionally a sea of red, so it was heartening to feel the energy in the room. We have to be passionate about every level of government." Amelia laughed. "When I lived in Canada I was never this involved in politics."

"And I never expected to be living in South Carolina again, or personally involved in stopping an American movement toward totalitarianism. Life surely is full of surprises."

"Let's hope there are more good surprises than bad in our futures."

CHAPTER 51

Edgar's and Rose's Luxury

A melia walked into the stunning marble lobby of the Mayflower Hotel on Connecticut Avenue in Washington, DC and joined the line of weary travelers waiting to check in at the front desk. She felt arms wrap around her from behind and let out a scream. She spun around to see her daughter staring at her.

"Mumma, it's me!" Lottie said as everyone in line turned to investigate the origin of the shriek. Amelia laughed, dropped her tote bag, and hugged her middle child.

"Sorry, Sweetheart. I guess I'm jumpy these days. I thought you were coming in later." Amelia picked up her bag and moved ahead in the line.

"I got an earlier flight, and I've been touring the city. I know we came here when I was young but I don't remember much of what we saw."

"It was in July, a hundred and five degrees, and humid. As I recall, you were all so grumpy that I'm not surprised you don't remember. Vacationing with children isn't always easy."

"I'm going to head up to my room. What time are we meeting your friend for dinner?"

"Come down to the lobby around seven. We can have a glass of wine before we meet Rose at seven thirty. Her friend Bruce is driving us to the restaurant."

"Great! I'll see you at seven."

Amelia watched her beautiful daughter walk to the elevators, turn, and wave like she did as a small child.

"Your daughter is lovely," said a woman standing in line behind her. "You must be Amelia Jones. I'm Jenna Prescott, Rose Windsor's publicist. She told me your daughter was joining us tonight. And she told me that the two of you look like sisters. It's true!"

"Nice to meet you, Jenna. I was happy when Rose invited me, and thrilled when I found out Lottie was coming too. Oh, it's my turn. I'll see you later."

Amelia checked in, then went to her room and unpacked. She pulled down the snowy white duvet and flopped onto the bed. She set the alarm on her phone to make certain she woke up in time to meet Lottie if she dozed off. Within minutes, she was in a deep sleep.

The alarm jolted her awake. She was disoriented, and glanced around at the cozy room in the historic hotel. When she got her bearings, she jumped up and took out her journal to record her dream. She didn't want the images to slip from her memory. The dream was similar to some of the visions she'd had since returning from the other side. She felt it was an important message.

Quickly, she dressed for dinner and sent a text to Michael saying she would be meeting Lottie in a few minutes. When she entered the hotel's opulent Edgar Bar and Restaurant, Lottie had two glasses of champagne waiting.

"I can't tell you how happy I am that you're here," Amelia began. "Let's toast to family, friends and women everywhere. Cheers."

"Cheers," Lottie chimed in as they tapped their flutes together. "Mum, I can't tell you how happy I am that you weren't hurt by that madman. That guy is seriously screwed up! Why do these people think they have the right to attack people in the name of God? Jeez."

"I don't know, Honey. I've been getting impressions about another conspiracy involving religious extremists. And I just had a dream that may relate to it. I was in the forest picking small, white trillium wildflowers. Every time I plucked one, one of the three petals dropped off. I could also smell incense, which was strange because I was in the woods! Incense always reminds me of the Catholic Church."

"Amelia!" a voice called from across the room. Rose was walking toward them, followed by a paunchy, middle-aged man with short-cropped hair and an amiable smile. Jenna trailed behind them. Introductions were swiftly made, and more champagne was ordered.

"Lottie, I've heard wonderful things about you. We need more passionate, involved young people to guide this country in the right direction," said Rose. "Or should I say, the *correct* direction."

"I know. So many people my age didn't bother to vote or wasted their vote on a fringe candidate. A multi-party system would be great, but in the meantime we can't let the alt-right run the country. At least that idiot HHS secretary quit. They should make him pay back the mil he wasted on private and military planes."

Amelia added, "I wish the Mueller investigation would hurry up and be completed, so we can force the psychopath out of office. I'm not sure the VP is any better, but at least he doesn't have a cult following."

"I copied some of the things Mueller might be working on," said Lottie. "Here, they're in the notes app on my phone. The charges could include obstruction of justice, violations of the Computer Fraud and Abuse Act, violations of the Federal Election Campaign Act dealing with fundraising, violations of the Foreign Agents Registration Act, violations of IRS and tax law, and money laundering. The list was compiled by a former assistant attorney general, under Bush."

"I pray they can make something stick," said Rose. "There are a number of speakers tomorrow at the forum who are going to address the legalities and escalating absurdity of this administration. Mercy, what a world!"

"The article went on to say: 'Keep in mind that Mueller cannot try T for any crimes he can prove the president committed. But he can make referrals to Congress, which then has the power to impeach the head of state. Mueller can also ask a grand jury to name T as an unindicted co-conspirator. This is the same thing that happened to Richard Nixon as a result of Watergate.'" Lottie put away her phone while everyone silently sipped the bubbly wine.

Amelia shook her head. "Therefore, it's still up to a Congress controlled by the Republicans to get him out of the White House, even if they can prove he's a criminal. What a system!"

Bruce looked at his watch, a Rolex, which had been a Christmas gift from Dr. Gabriel. His breath caught in his throat, then he shook his head and recovered his composure. When he'd arrived earlier, he was surprised to see that the hotel bar was named Edgar and the restaurant they were going to that evening was called Rose's Luxury. It was like the universe was telling him he was in the right place at the right time. Dr. Gabriel would be joining him at the hotel later that evening.

"Time to go, ladies. The valet is bringing around the car."

Amelia perceived the aura around Bruce and was concerned. She'd never experienced the erratic flashes of red and grey that shot through his energy field. She'd ask Rose about him later.

They strolled out into the cool night air, then loaded everyone into Bruce's white SUV for the drive to Rose's Luxury. None of them had been there before, but the reviews were excellent. The charming restaurant lived up to their expectations.

CHAPTER 52

Slush Fund

D r. Gabriel used the burner phone to tell Father Rathbone that he would be in DC for three nights, and it was a good opportunity for them to meet again in person. They decided to leave Miller out of the equation for the moment. Josh had been harassing Edgar about his former-CIA contact and the advice on administering a deadly drug. There was something unnerving in the Reverend's demeanor that upset the doctor.

Gabriel and Rathbone had talked about changing the KNC from a trio to a duo if Josh's behavior became any more erratic. The father had originally been worried about Gabriel and the black ops connection, but Miller's raving texts in the middle of the night were even more concerning. Sometimes Josh seemed as unhinged as man in the Oval Office. Henry wondered if it was a symptom of malignant narcissism or the sociopathic tendencies exhibited by 45 and by Josh. Whatever the origin of Miller's disturbed ranting's, Henry didn't want events spiraling out of his control. Ultimately, they decided to leave things as they were, but wanted to limit the communication with Miller.

Father Rathbone found an inexpensive motel in the DC area. He used a secret Opus Dei slush fund for his flight to Reagan Airport, the motel, and a rental car. His intention was to finalize the actions by Robert and the ex-CIA hit man on both targets. Political power had to remain in the hands of the right and righteous Republicans, whether T was in office or not.

Father Rathbone texted Sophia, saying he was going out of town on Church business. He'd miss their tryst during his time away but he'd make it up to her upon his return. He was confident that God would forgive his carnal pleasures when Henry ensured that Christianity and the Catholic Church would be at the forefront of the movement to keep and expand religion in the halls of power.

CHAPTER 53

Womens Forum

L ottie and Amelia met for breakfast the following morning. The horrendous mass shooting the night before in Nevada had shaken them both to the core. They talked about the heartbreaking tragedy first. Then they reviewed the various seminars at the forum held at several locations at George Washington University in DC, including the Jack Morton Auditorium and larger Lisner Auditorium.

"My gosh," said Amelia. "There are so many challenges facing our country. Look at this list of topics: Sexual Harassment and the #MeToo Movement; Women of Color and White Supremacy; Fascism in the 21st Century; Moms and the Opioid Epidemic; Feminism—a Phoenix Rising; Defending Mother Earth from Climate Change and Pruitt's EPA; The Media and Authoritarianism; and Narcissistic Personality Disorder in the Oval Office."

"I was just reading about the MeToo movement. There are a couple of others I want to attend: one on the Native American Women's Movement, and one presented by Harvard's center on early education and at-risk children." Lottie pulled up the website on her phone and read, "'The Center on the Developing Child's R&D platform, supports scientific research that can inform the testing, implementation, and refinement of strategies designed to achieve significantly better life outcomes for children facing adversity.'"

"It sounds right up your alley, Lottie. That type of innovation is what we need, not the horrific destruction of public education by the secretary of education. The fact that she has rescinded the protections for transgender students, sexual assault survivors, and wants to take away rights for disabled students is horrible! She's self-serving and malevolent, like many others in the Cabinet who are trying to destroy government agencies."

"Oh, time to go to the session that Rose is part of," added Lottie.

The Lisner Auditorium was filled to capacity. The organizers regretted not securing the much larger Smith Center for the event, since they had quickly surpassed the 1500 participants needed to fill the auditorium. Rose was seated onstage with three leading voices in the women's movement. Instead of the usual welcome, the first speaker, Olivia Atkinson addressed the issue on everyone's mind.

"Good morning, and welcome. I will not ask for a moment of silence. We have been silent too long. I will not be sending my prayers to the families of the murdered and those injured at the concert in Las Vegas; I'll be sending letters and emails to the NRA and the Republican and Democratic members of Congress demanding they end the insanity. No citizen needs automatic or semi-automatic weapons of war for personal protection or hunting."

Loud applause came from the audience. Olivia continued.

"The formidable gun culture in the United States has led to two hundred seventy-three mass shootings this year alone. What will it take for the voice of the majority who want sensible gun laws to get their elected officials to stand up to the NRA and other lobbyists? We are not a civilized country if we allow tens of thousands of people to die every year because of gun violence."

Voices cheered in agreement. The trauma the of fifty-plus killed and over 500 injured at a country music festival in Las Vegas had shocked the nation. The fact that one lone gunman could carry out such carnage was devastating. The fact that he obtained dozens of weapons legally, and that bump stalks could turn semi-automatic into automatic guns, was more than any sane person could bear.

"It's time for the Wild West to be relegated to the pages of history. When there are more guns than people in a nation, there's something seriously wrong. This was clearly an act of domestic terrorism. And the NRA and Republicans in Congress say this isn't the time to talk about control. If not now, when?" There was more applause.

Olivia continued. "Our first speaker today is from a Southern state where the gun lobby is very strong. Dr. Rose Windsor has written extensively on feminism in the South and the future of women in red states. Please extend her a warm welcome."

Polite applause greeted Rose. "Thank you, Olivia. I'm honored to be here today. Sensible gun laws. That isn't what I was going to speak about today, but not addressing the horrific events in Las Vegas would be inexcusable. I don't own a gun but almost every member of my extended family does. I'm not against their right to do so under the Second Amendment, but the worship of weapons is like a religious experience to many Americans, and changing that paradigm will be difficult.

"South Carolina has many wonderful attributes. The traditions and gentility of the South, along with a strong sense of community, are some of the things I admire about my home. But we suffer from disavowal of our history of slavery and its continuing impact on society. The strength of Southern women is undeniable, yet both women's and men's support of misogyny has gone on far too long.

"One thing my Southern parents insisted on was honesty. When you have a man in the Oval Office who has outright lied or misrepresented over one thousand, three hundred times since January 20, 2017, this country is in dire straits. A pathological liar whose supporters ignore his lies or spin the truth is dangerous."

Rose spoke for another twenty minutes. Lottie, Amelia, Jenna, and Bruce were seated in the third row. Amelia kept glancing at Bruce who fidgeted nonstop. He bounced his legs and folded and unfolded his program. He was obviously barely holding it together. The moment Rose's presentation was over; Bruce jumped up and bolted out of the hall.

CHAPTER 54

Our Biases

That evening, Jenna left for New York, and Bruce wasn't answering his phone. Rose made arrangements to meet Amelia and Lottie for dinner. The conversation quickly turned to the ongoing plight of the people in Puerto Rico.

"I believe the Federal Government is not responding like they did to the hurricanes in Florida and Texas because the majority of Puerto Ricans are Hispanic. It will be a long time before the power grid is back up and water is plentiful," said Rose. "45's disgusting publicity stunt, when he threw rolls of paper towels at evacuees and personally attacked the mayor of San Juan, is unconscionable."

"The daily assault on democracy, like when T wants to shut down the media if they criticize him, along with the other nefarious actions by his oligarchy, is almost unbearable. I guess that's what they're counting on—intellectual and emotional fatigue," said Lottie. "Divide and conquer. How do we get past this and make things better?"

"I wonder what the future holds for such a divided nation," added Rose.

Amelia pulled out her phone. "Ben sent me this *New York Times* article by conservative writer Peter Wehner. It's about how each side seeks validation of their beliefs. 'Confirmation bias is deepening political polarization, which is already at record levels. Our political culture is sick and getting sicker, and confirmation bias is now a leading toxin.'"

"So, Mum, what kind of doctor can heal the country?"

"I'm not sure, Sweetie, but he went on to say there should be 'greater appreciation for the perspectives of the other side. We have to look within and see ourselves and our limitation with fresh eyes.' It reminded me of what Linda said to me during my NDE about seeing with our spiritual eyes."

Lottie laughed. "He even mentioned the other side, although he didn't mean the spirit world."

"I know, I thought that was funny. He finished with: 'Objective reality exists, truth matters, and we have to pursue them with purpose and without fear. But in our present moment, truth, including truth that unsettles us, has far too often become subordinate to justify and defend at all costs our own, often unsound perceptions.'"

"Truth does matter," added Rose. "That was a point I was making today."

"Ben is good at finding interesting articles. He's cool for a little brother," said Lottie.

"And Sasha always sends me thought-provoking scientific articles and books. My children keep me well informed." Amelia paused. "Only light and love can dispel the dark. I finally remembered another thing Linda said. Imagine if each cause was represented by a candle—no, something brighter, like a lantern. No one issue was more important, or light was brighter, than the other. But when people came together in unity, bringing all the lanterns, a single point could become a flood of light, dispelling the darkness."

"Like the Women's March on January 21st and all the other marches and sit-ins and protests," said Rose. "And one group can take the lead at a specific moment and be supported by the whole, like the protests at the airports after the Muslim ban."

"Yeah, we can back each other up as women and citizens," Lottie said.

"Love and light, will unite. Maybe then, we could become a beacon for those in the political middle and the discouraged right. With humility, compassion and open hearts we could reach across the aisle."

"That's profound, Mumma. Your trip to the world beyond has brought wisdom."

Amelia smiled. The three women sipped their wine and nibbled on appetizers as they processed the ideas.

"This administration has, at the least, created a nation of psychology students. That session today on Narcissistic Personality Disorder was enlightening. Will all this awareness of mental disorders help us navigate this reality?" Rose asked. "Will it enable us to resist the movement toward authoritarianism?"

Rose received a text. "It's from Bruce. He's sorry he couldn't join us for dinner."

"Is he OK, Rose? I saw a disturbance in his aura and this morning I thought he was going to jump out of his skin."

"I've noticed there's something wrong too. But he won't talk to me about it. We've been friends for so long, and it's upsetting that he won't confide in me. Speaking of disorders, he's bipolar—and it's getting worse."

"Isn't he involved with someone at Freedom University?" asked Amelia.

"Yes, his 'friend' is one of the most prominent religious figures there. They've had a secret relationship for many years. Maybe there's a problem between the men," said Rose.

"We all have our personal problems to deal with, as well as intense societal difficulties," said Lottie. "It's a test of our fortitude as individuals and as a nation."

Amelia smiled. "Rose, do you want me to ask Bruce to tell the truth?"

"Not at this point. I hadn't even thought of using your special ability to understand what's happening. Thanks anyway."

"It must be so hard for Bruce to keep a secret like that. Thank goodness most in my generation are fine with people loving whomever they want. Life is tough enough," Lottie added.

"I wish all evangelical leaders would embrace same-sex partnerships, and healthcare for all, and renewable energy and reproductive rights for women... I wish they'd bring religion into the 21st century," Rose stated.

"Let's drink to that!"

CHAPTER 55

The Crash

Sophia! Why would Robert do that without my permission? He's ruined everything!" Father Rathbone yelled into the phone.

"Henry, I'm so sorry. He got carried away. Please forgive him," answered Sophia.

"We'll talk when I get back." The father threw the phone on the bed and paced around the motel room like a caged animal. He turned on the television to a local news station. There it was; the governor of Virginia had crashed his car into a concrete barrier. He'd been taken to a Richmond hospital near the state capital. The police were investigating the cause of the crash on one of the governor's frequent late-night trips to White Castle. His condition was unknown at the present time.

"That idiot! I shouldn't have trusted someone so unstable. What was I thinking?" Henry yelled at the walls.

He decided to keep his meeting with Dr. Gabriel at The Mayflower bar. He grabbed his coat and jumped into the rental car. Arriving at the hotel, he valeted the car and surveyed the lobby making certain he didn't recognize anyone. He was more paranoid than ever.

The doctor was swirling his scotch on the rocks at the bar, and a second glass of the golden liquid was waiting for the priest. Unbeknown to the men, Bruce was watching from a table in the dining room. He was out of earshot but closely observed them as the religious leaders spoke in hushed voices with heads close together. In a near panic, Bruce threw cash on the table and slipped out of the restaurant. He rushed to the valet stand to call for his vehicle.

"Jesus H. Christ!" said Gabriel. "Is he dead?"

"I don't know. Robert had been following his moves when the governor drove his own car. He saw a pattern in the evenings and took it upon himself to put the plan in motion. God knows what we should do now."

"Did you speak to Miller?" asked Edgar. "His texts are bizarre."

"Yes, and I agree he's becoming a liability. Maybe we should shut this down for now. There's still a lot of time before the midterm elections. No one will know that we had anything to do with the governor. I can assure you, Robert will be under my control from now on," said Henry.

The men finished their scotch, shook hands, and left the bar. Father Rathbone got his car from the valet and drove back to the motel. He turned to the local TV news station to see if there was an update on the governor, but there was no additional information. What Rathbone didn't know was that Bruce had tailed him.

CHAPTER 56

Duty to Warn

A melia and Lottie met for breakfast the following morning. "How did you sleep, Honey?" Amelia asked.

"Pretty good, how about you?"

"Not great," Amelia answered. "I had a nightmare about hands around my neck choking the life out of me. Every traumatic event has consequences. I spent years after my abduction having horrible dreams. Your poor dad was woken up many times with my screaming."

"Trauma to one person affects so many loved ones, too. Mum, what is going on in this country? It's an inferno in Napa Valley with too much death and destruction. Are there more natural disasters like the wildfires right now? Is it a physical manifestation of the political madness?"

"Climate change is contributing to the intensity of the disasters. I feel terrible for those poor people who've lost their homes and neighborhoods, and those who didn't survive the flames," said Amelia.

"I doubt 45 will have any compassion for Californians—oh wait, he isn't capable of compassion and doesn't have a conscience. Psychopath."

"I was reading an article in *The New Yorker* magazine this morning about a new book called *The Dangerous Case of D T: 27 Psychiatrists and Mental Health Experts Assess a President*. The Duty to Warn group of professionals wrote it. They assert that T is a dangerous, malignant narcissist completely unfit for office."

Lottie sipped her coffee. "So how does that help the situation?"

"The group is creating a Twenty-Fifth Amendment PAC to raise money for candidates to run on the issue of establishing an Oversight Commission on Presidential Capacity. According to the Twenty-fifth Amendment, the congress can either have the vice president and a majority of cabinet members begin impeachment proceedings, or Congress can set up a commission."

"Cool! That gives me hope," answered Lottie.

"These people are standing up for what's right even though they could be jeopardizing their careers. They're going against protocol and could risk being disciplined by the licensing boards."

"Oh, it's time to go, Mum. We're supposed to meet Rose before the first session."

The women joined Rose outside the auditorium. There were ripples of conversation about the governor of Virginia being in a car accident.

"Rose, what happened to the governor?" Amelia asked.

"From what I've heard, he was in a serious crash last night. It seems he lost control of the car and smashed into a concrete barrier. He's in the hospital, but I don't know the status of his condition."

"Doesn't he have a driver?" Lottie questioned.

"Usually, but it's well known that he makes late-night fast-food runs and drives himself," answered Rose. "Bruce has mentioned it before."

Entering the room with the flow of the crowd, Rose scanned the area for Bruce. She finally spotted him and waved him over. Once again, Rose got the impression that Bruce was distracted and disturbed. She hoped her friend wasn't unraveling. They found seats together in the back of the auditorium.

Once they were seated, Amelia closed her eyes. A wave of energy washed over her. Lottie gently touched her arm and Amelia opened her eyes.

"What is it, Mum?"

"It wasn't his fault. Somehow the governor's car was tampered with. Again, I'm getting the impression of a trillium wildflower and the smell of incense, as if there's a religious connection."

"How do you know that?" asked Bruce. "I don't understand the power you claim you have. Are you sure?"

"We'll have to talk about this later, Amelia. The speakers are about to begin," said Rose.

After the final session of the morning, Lottie said she wanted to tour the capital city and finish with the International Spy Museum. Amelia was going to remain at George Washington University, then meet her daughter at the corner of Jackson Place and Pennsylvania Avenue at 7 p.m. Rose told them she was heading for the airport to return to South Carolina, and Bruce said he wasn't certain of his plans.

During the afternoon sessions, Amelia chatted with other participants about the latest news on the Virginia governor and it was confirmed that he was expected to recover. There was no information about the cause of the crash. Amelia was still puzzled by her intuitive impressions. There were also discussions about the humiliating lack of attendees at the VP's rally in a red part of Virginia the past weekend. The VP was there on behalf of a Republican gubernatorial candidate and the small, unenthusiastic crowd illustrated that the vice president lacked the cult appeal of his boss.

At the end of the day, Amelia gathered her things and began to walk to the meeting place with her daughter. She strolled along H Street past The World Bank building. The evening was cool and clear, and Amelia was feeling energized by the discussions of the day. For the first time since the election, she had hope for the future. She believed there were enough good citizens to turn the tide in 2018 and bring rational, coherent, and sane leadership to the Federal Government.

Amelia heard her phone chime and pulled it out of her purse. Lottie had sent a text that she'd be 10 minutes late. Amelia typed OK, and dropped the phone in her jacket pocket.

CHAPTER 57

Stake Out

During the afternoon, Bruce staked out the motel where he'd followed Edgar's acquaintance the previous evening. He was considering his options on how to approach the man. He had to know if there was a physical relationship between Dr. Gabriel and the stranger. Bruce was feeling manic, to the point that he could barely sit in the car. He loaded and unloaded the pistol in his hands, deciding if he should use the weapon to threaten the man if he refused to talk.

The stranger pulled into the motel parking lot just before 6:00 and went into the room. Bruce continued to debate what his next move should be and exited the car. He paced back and forth several times, then shouted, "I've got it!" He jumped back into the vehicle and drove away. He made his way through traffic and began to circle the White House, looking for the one person whose help he was desperate to enlist.

A short time later, Bruce saw his target walking down Pennsylvania Avenue. He waited until she crossed the intersection and entered the park across from the White House. Amelia looked toward 1600 Pennsylvania Avenue and saw softly glowing, multi-colored lights swirling over the building. *Oh my gosh! It looks like an aura above the White House. There's a dark grey vortex in one area like a mini black hole. 45 must be in the Oval Office,* she thought.

In the growing dusk, Amelia turned and faced the General Rochambeau statue, watching the passersby. She imagined the life of the people walking past—this one was a tourist, the next was a low-level government staffer, and the one striding briskly by her was CIA.

She didn't notice the vehicle pull up on the lawn behind her, but spun around when she heard the engine. She was shocked to see Bruce jump out of the car, run around the front of the vehicle, and open the front passenger door.

"Bruce, what are you doing?"

"I need your help. Please get in the car. Right now."

"I'm sorry, I can't. I'm meeting Lottie here."

"I can't wait!" he yelled. "Get in, now."

Bruce grabbed Amelia's arm and dragged her to the car door. She fought him off and almost tumbled to the ground. He gripped her again, took the pistol from his pocket and aimed it at Amelia. She was shocked at the sight of a weapon. He shoved her toward the front seat and threw her into the car. He snatched her purse and tossed it into the far backseat. With tires squealing, he floored the engine. Grass and dirt flew in the air as he sped away.

From across the park, Lottie ran at full speed. She was horrified to see her mother being abducted and forced into a white SUV.

"Stop! Mum!" Lottie screamed.

CHAPTER 58

Confession

A melia stared straight ahead and tried not to hyperventilate. *Breathe, just breathe. It's going to be fine. I know this man won't hurt me. I pray he won't hurt me! He's frightened and distressed. I won't do anything to make him pull the trigger.*

She had surreptitiously slipped her right hand into her pocket and turned off the ringer on her phone. She didn't want Bruce to know it was with her, and not in her purse in the back of the SUV.

They drove in silence through the growing darkness. Bruce kept the gun in his right hand, visible but not aimed directly at his passenger. Finally, they pulled into a motel parking lot and stopped at the far end under a flickering street lamp.

Bruce turned off the engine and rocked back and forth in his seat. Amelia sat stiffly beside him, trying to decide if she should attempt escape or play along. She knew that Bruce was battling a mental disorder and she didn't want to do something to push him off the deep end. Then she heard a voice in her head stating, *remain calm.*

OK, Linda. What should I do? she asked in her mind. The answer came quickly: *your phone.* Amelia felt for her phone in her pocket. While Bruce continued to rock, she carefully turned on her phone and hit the recording app. It was just in the nick of time. Bruce suddenly opened the car door and demanded that she get out and follow him.

Bruce pushed Amelia in front of him and held the gun in the small of her back. They walked to room nine and Bruce pounded on the cheap wooden door. A man opened the door wide, not expecting a hostile stranger on the other side.

"Can I help you?" asked Father Rathbone.

Bruce shoved Amelia into the priest and displayed the pistol. "Get inside," he hissed. They all moved into the room and Bruce slammed the door behind him.

"What in God's name are you doing?" Father Rathbone yelled. He looked at Bruce then at Amelia, standing frozen in place.

"Shut up. It's what *you're* doing. What's your relationship to Edgar? I saw you at the bar. And you've been talking to him on a secret phone. Are you two having an affair?"

"No, no!" Henry said as he backed away from the gun. "It's just business. We're not personally involved."

Bruce waved the gun around and Amelia moved away to stay out of the line of fire.

"Who are you? What business?" Bruce growled.

"I'm Henry Rathbone, a Catholic priest from Jacksonville. Edgar and I met at the RNC convention last January. We're—we're working together on a project to save Christianity. That's all!"

"You're lying. Edgar wouldn't work with a Catholic priest."

"It's true!"

Bruce paced back and forth in front of Rathbone, then stopped. In a calmer voice he began, "I knew you'd lie to me. That's why I brought my insurance policy."

He grabbed Amelia's arm and pulled her close. "Do it, Mrs. Jones. Do your thing."

Amelia took a deep breath to calm her nerves. She finally understood what was driving Bruce to this madness—his insecurity and jealousy. Henry stared at her, not comprehending what was going on. Amelia felt a wave of female warrior energy flow through her body and yanked her arm out of Bruce's grasp. She boldly stepped before the priest.

"What is your relationship to Dr. Gabriel?" she asked. "Father Rathbone, the truth be told."

Henry began to shake. Sweat formed on his forehead and he gasped for air. "I swear we're not physically involved. Dr. Gabriel, Reverend Josh Miller and I formed the KNC, the Knights of the New Crusade. We're determined to ensure that the progress made by the Republicans in government isn't destroyed by the Godless left."

Amelia gasped and stepped back in shock at the mention of the KNC. Now she wanted answers as much as Bruce.

"Father, what were your plans?" she said. "The truth be told."

Henry shuddered at the shock going through his body and tried hard not to answer, but to no avail.

"We have to safeguard Christianity! Even if the president is removed from office we can't let the heathens gain control again. We contrived to eliminate three top Democratic contenders for 2020. We had to take matters into our own hands, regardless of the personal cost!"

"That's insane," said Amelia. "Why do you think you'll frighten Democrats and stop them from running?"

"If we murdered three of them, the best of the other candidates would be intimidated and fear running for the presidency. Then the Republicans would retain the White House."

"Who are the targets?" she demanded.

"I can't, I won't tell you!" the priest yelled.

"The truth be told, Father."

In a strained voice he declared, "The female senator from Northern California will get a sniper's bullet to the head, the young congressman from Massachusetts will be poisoned, and the Virginia governor was supposed to perish in a car crash."

There was a look of terror on Henry's face; he realized he must stop these two from leaving the room. He rushed at Bruce and grabbed the gun. The men struggled and a shot was fired, narrowly missing Amelia's head.

"Run, Amelia!" Bruce screamed as he wrestled with the priest.

She rushed out the door and bolted across the parking lot toward the motel office. As another shot rang out, she looked back at room nine to make sure the priest wasn't following her. Amelia didn't see the Mini Cooper speeding into the lot directly into her path. With a thud, she bounced off the hood of the car and landed in a heap on the pavement.

CHAPTER 59

Blame

"Mumma, wake up. I know you can hear me," said Lottie. She was holding her mother's hand as she sat beside the hospital bed.

"We're all here, my darling. Sasha and Lottie and Ben," added Michael. Each member of the Jones family was distraught at the sight of Amelia, once again unresponsive after an accident. They gathered around the bed and gently placed their hands on the woman they loved so much.

Slowly, Amelia opened her eyes and looked at the worried faces around her.

"What...what happened?"

They all cheered. "You were hit by a car and have been unconscious for almost two days," said Michael as he kissed her forehead.

"Not again," said Amelia and touched the bandage on her head. "I'm not sure how much more abuse my poor brain can take."

"I'm not sure how much more stress my heart can take," Michael said. "I'm not letting you out of my sight for a long time."

"We promise to see you more often, Mom. You don't have to keep getting into accidents to bring us all together," Sasha added with a smile.

"Bruce! Is he OK?"

"He was shot in the leg by that priest, but he's going to pull through. They arrested Bruce for armed kidnapping," answered Ben. "Lottie gave the police Bruce's name and the make of his SUV. An APB was put out on his car. The guy who hit you and the motel manager called 911 and police were there in minutes. They said the priest drove away, but he yelled out the window that someone was injured in room nine."

"And the father?"

"They tracked him down in Florida," said Sasha. "He used a false name at the hotel, but used his real name for the car rental and flight."

Amelia bolted upright then flopped back onto the pillow. "But what about the conspiracy? What about the KNC?"

"Bruce didn't say a word about it, probably because he didn't want to implicate Dr. Gabriel," added Lottie. "He told them it was a personal conflict with Rathbone. But once the police listened to the recording on your phone, everything changed. You nailed them, Mumma. That was quick thinking to record them."

"It was Linda who whispered in my ear to use my phone. Oh my God! The Virginia governor—was the KNC responsible for his accident?"

"They've launched a full investigation into Father Rathbone, Dr. Gabriel, and the other man," stated Ben. "They're following up with the Virginia police, looking into the crash. They're confident those religious lunatics were involved. It looks like the car's computer was hijacked."

"I hope the police don't release my name and connection to all this."

Michael pulled up a chair, sat beside his wife, and held her hand. "Don't worry. I've spoken with the local law enforcement and the FBI. They've agreed to keep your name out of the public report. Your mishap with the Mini Cooper will be listed as a pedestrian accident."

"Poor Bruce. His actions were caused by his mental disorder. Rose must be distraught about what he did."

"I talked to Rose," added Lottie. "She feels awful, and hopes you'll be OK. She's worried you'll blame her for not seeing the danger you were in."

"She couldn't have known Bruce would have a meltdown and kidnap me at gunpoint. Again, my vision was off—it wasn't a white van, but a white SUV that I was forced into."

"But you were right that it was in front of the White House," said Michael.

Amelia took a glass from the table and sipped the cool water. She closed her eyes and thought about everything she'd been through since the paddleboard incident.

"Mom, did you have another spiritual adventure when you were unconscious?" asked Sasha.

Amelia opened her eyes. "Yes, something happened—but I can't recall exactly what. It will probably take some time to fit the pieces of the puzzle together. And I'm not sure I still have my psychic ability."

CHAPTER 60

Sunrise

Henry Rathbone caught the last flight to Jacksonville. He picked up his car and drove to the Opus Dei office in Jax Beach. He spent the night writing letters to the bishop, his brother, and Sophia. To the bishop he expressed his regret for failing as a Knight for God and defending the gains made under the current administration. He was worried that the presidency would implode and the GOP would fracture, allowing the opposition to gain control in 2020.

He detailed the KNC's origins and activities, and despaired that their plans would never be realized. He feared for the future of the traditional Catholic Church, under the current pope and in the present political climate. He asked the bishop to hire a lawyer for Sophia and Robert. He insisted that he coerced them and the church must help with their defenses.

To his brother he wrote about his gratitude for ending the violence by their father. He wished him a long and happy life. Henry told Ted that in his heart of hearts he didn't believe the Church's dogma on eternal damnation. He believed that God would ultimately forgive his sins after the appropriate atonement following his physical death.

In his letter to Sophia, he forgave Robert for his disastrous action. He thanked her for her loyalty, and said he would always love her and cherish their time together. He asked for her forgiveness in getting her and Robert involved with the conspiracy, and told her the bishop would assist in their defense. He gave her a final blessing and hoped she would find a good man and have a family.

Finally, Henry wrote a note confessing his involvement in the KNC and revealed the scheme and its participants. He unlocked a metal box and took out an antique seal and a stick of wax. He placed the letter in an envelope, lit the stick, and watched the blood red wax drip onto the back of the envelope. He firmly pressed the brass seal into the wax. Then he retrieved another item out of the metal box and dropped it in his pocket.

Just before dawn, he posted the letters and drove north to Atlantic Beach. He parked, slowly walked to the ocean's edge, and removed his sandals. He waded into the cool water as the sun began to rise over the horizon. It was a magnificent sunrise, with glorious shades of pink and gold in the scattered clouds. Sunlight glinted on the gentle waves rolling to the shore. Tears rolled down his face, as he gazed on his final sunrise.

Several people strolled behind him, taking photos of the dawn. When they had passed, he took a revolver from his pocket. His brother had given him the weapon years earlier.

In a clear, steady voice he said, "Father, forgive me for I have sinned. Please absolve me of my past transgressions and the one I am about to commit."

Father Henry Rathbone placed the gun to his temple and pulled the trigger.

CHAPTER 61

Headlines

The warm afternoon sun poured down on Amelia as she sat on the lanai, recording her musings and memories in a notebook. The mallard ducks and their now-grown offspring glided across the pond. A small white rabbit hopped along the back of the yard, reminding her of the strange journey she'd been on.

It had been many weeks since the accident, and it was taking her a long time to remember the events on the other side. The screen door opened and Lyla joined her.

"Hey, my friend. Michael let me in. How are you doing?"

"Pretty, pretty good, as Larry David would say."

Lyla chuckled and dropped into a chair. "It was a shame to hear about the Jax priest who committed suicide. Thank goodness the FBI arrested his co-conspirators in that crazy scheme to assassinate the top Dems."

"And I'm grateful they kept my name out of the whole sordid affair."

"What are you writing about?"

"Things I remember from my second coma. And about bridges—the invisible kind—the ones we must create to reach across the political divide. If we build them, maybe open-minded people on the other side of the aisle will meet us halfway."

"Did you come to that conclusion when you were unconscious?"

"No," Amelia answered. "It was the KNC conspiracy that made me realize how dangerous the political climate has become. It's like swirling black clouds in a green-tinged sky that at any moment can turn into a tornado. The fact that religious leaders felt they had to murder top Democratic figures is beyond comprehension."

"You're right. Fanatics on both sides have been given license to act in the most extreme ways. What makes someone cross the line of human decency and threaten another's life? People have done horrible things in the name of God and country for thousands of years, so I guess it shouldn't be a surprise."

"Isn't it incredible how the nation has turned on a dime. Or should I say, an election."

"And the deplorable head of the EPA, who's hell-bent on polluting the environment and endangering citizens' health in the name of corporate profit, has received death threats. That's not the answer."

"You're correct, Lyla. More violence isn't the answer."

"There's a certain part of the population that will never give up their cult following of T. They thrive on chaos and conflict."

"45's fights with the families of fallen soldiers are unreal. He simply can't stop lying, let any criticism go, or apologize when he's wrong. And that lying, sycophantic poodle, aka the VP, who gazes adoringly at T... It's so disturbing," Amelia added.

"Where is this all leading?" Lyla questioned. "Too many in Congress have sold their souls to the devil in the Oval Office. I wish the path to bridging the gap was clearer."

"And yet the Democratic victories in the November 8th elections are heartening. It was great that Virginia, New Jersey, and Washington State all swung left. That's what gives me hope."

The women sat in silence for a while. "Isn't it amazing how many women—and men—have started to speak out about sexual harassment and attacks involving so many powerful men? Heads of studios, famous directors, actors, politicians and TV personalities are all being accused," said Amelia. "As well as business leaders and others in positions of power. And political affiliation makes no difference. The MeToo movement is barreling down the track like a runaway train."

"And the best news of all is the Democratic victory in the Alabama Senate race. Decency and the votes of black women led to the victory over the accused pedophile. It was discouraging how many women in Alabama said they didn't believe the victims, or didn't care if the Republican candidate is an accused child molester."

"Females have been harassed forever. But maybe the tide will turn, and abusers will get the message that this has to end. And companies and the government will take responsibility for what goes on in the workplace."

Lyla added, "There's bound to be a backlash, but I believe this worldwide movement will keep progressing."

"I'll definitely include this seismic shift in my novel."

"Have you started writing?" Lyla asked.

"Not yet. Slowly, I've been recovering my memories of when I was unconscious after bouncing off the Mini Cooper. Linda was there and she reminded me to see the world through my spiritual eyes. Then she led me into a darkened theater. I was worried I was going to see The Magician again! Instead, a young girl strolled down the aisle, sat beside me, and held my hand. I knew she was my future granddaughter."

"How exciting, Amelia. Will she be your first grandchild?"

"I'm not sure. I have a feeling my first grandbaby will be a boy. I also got the impression that when I returned, I would no longer have the ability to make people tell the truth, but the torch would be passed to my granddaughter. Her gift will be different—people would instinctively be honest when they were around her."

"Is that a relief?"

"Yes and no. My fifteen minutes of fame were hard, but I did enjoy helping people and solving mysteries. I also felt that when I returned I'd have precognition, the capability to see what might happen in the future. A new twist to the story."

"Amazing. What else did you see in the theater?"

"The movie screen lit up, and I saw scenes of what I instinctively knew were possible future scenarios. Each one began with a newspaper headline. Nothing was set in stone, but I believe the scenes represented what could happen. Here, you can read about what I saw."

Amelia handed her notebook to her friend, then leaned back and closed her eyes. Lyla began to read.

"1. Headline: 'Final Arrest in Russia Case Reaches the White House.' After several of T's campaign and administration members were indicted on charges of perjury, collusion with a foreign enemy, money laundering and obstruction of *justice, the special prosecutor went to the White House. The VP was indicted for perjury and obstruction of justice in relation to the cover-ups of Russian involvement with 45's administration. The stock market plummeted based on the news.*

2. Headline: 'Massive Stroke Takes Down T.' There was a scene of T in a wheelchair, partially paralyzed and drooling. He was staring at a television when his first wife entered. She took the phone out of his hand, turned off the TV, and began to humiliate him in retaliation for the misery he'd caused her and her children. She taunted him, asking if God had given him the stroke, if it was the KGB now called the FSB, or if it had been a homegrown black ops attack by someone who was hired to protect him.

3. Headline: 'VP Shot Down in Afghanistan.' The scene showed a smiling vice president on a visit to Afghanistan. A missile struck the airport in the capital city of Kabul, and the VP was quickly put into a helicopter to get him to a safe location. As they were taking off, a ground-to-air missile struck the chopper and it exploded, leaving no survivors. The scene shifted to a prison television room. Alton Fry was watching the news on the VP's death. He jumped up and started yelling that God had worked his magic and the Speaker would be president. Guards quickly subdued Fry."

Lyla put down the notebook and touched Amelia's arm.

"Oh, my God. Will any of this come true?" asked Lyla.

"Time will tell. It's interesting that there were two possible scenarios for the VP—one in which he was heading to prison, and the other in which he was killed. I forgot to tell you, an FBI agent called to say they found the Secret Service member of The Deacons who murdered the guy in DC and was planning to eliminate the VP. Thank goodness that's over with."

Michael joined the women.

"What's up, Honey?"

"Just watching 45 on TV. He won't take any responsibility for anything he says or does. Soon he'll reach two thousand lies or misleading statements. It's mindboggling! Hopefully, his debasement of American society will end with the Democrats gaining power in 2018 and 2020."

Lyla added, "And the special counsel has already indicted several people associated with the 2016 campaign. Maybe Amelia's correct that others will be charged, and the political winds will shift in a new direction."

"Then we can build a bridge to a brighter future," said Amelia.

EPILOGUE

2/21/21

A melia Jones was ushered into the Oval Office. The door closed silently behind her. She took a moment to look around the historic room, and spotted a figure by one of the tall windows framed by pale blue drapes. A woman was standing there very still, peering out into the moonlight.

"Excuse me, Senator—oh sorry, I mean Madam President," Amelia said.

The president turned around and walked over to her guest. She wore an elegant navy suit and her signature strand of pearls. Her smile was warm and genuine.

"Mrs. Jones, I'm so happy to meet you. Until I read the confidential files on the Knights of the New Crusade, I had no knowledge of your role in the affair. I wanted to thank you for your service to the country, to me personally and to the vice president. The conspirators were on the mark with two of us ending up in the White House. Fortunately, the former governor fully recovered from his accident. I was grateful he could join my Cabinet."

Amelia blushed as she shook the president's hand. "Thank you. It's such a pleasure to meet you. I can't tell you how thrilled I am that you're the resident of this Office. You and the vice president ran a brilliant campaign. And thank goodness that African-Americans, Hispanics and millennials showed up and voted."

"Not only did they vote, record numbers of young people, women, and ethnically diverse citizens ran for office and won," the President added.

"Please, have a seat and tell me how this came about. I remember seeing you on social media several years ago."

Settling into the cream-colored sofa, Amelia began her extraordinary story. "Well, it all started when I was hit on the head by a paddleboard..."

THE END

About the Author

PHOTO BY BECKY JAQUES HASAK

Originally from Toronto, Canada, this is Louise Jaques' third novel set on Amelia Island, FL. In *Dreams of Amelia*, a psychic young woman's new romance and ultimately her life are threatened by a dangerous nemesis from a past lifetime. In *Splitters, An Amelia Island Mystery*, four women become amateur sleuths, as they're swept up in the investigation of a millionaire's murder. Louise and her husband, Mike split their time between Amelia Island and St. Louis, MO. They are excited to welcome their first grandchild.

You can reach Louise at louise.jaques@hotmail.com.